A Father for Daisy

A Father for Daisy

Karen Abbott

ROBERT HALE · LONDON

© Karen Abbott 2011
First published in Great Britain 2011

ISBN 978-0-7090-9241-4

Robert Hale Limited
Clerkenwell House
Clerkenwell Green
London EC1R 0HT

www.halebooks.com

2 4 6 8 10 9 7 5 3 1

Typeset in 10.75/16pt New Century Schoolbook
Printed in Great Britain by the MPG Books Group,
Bodmin and King's Lynn

I dedicate 'A Father For Daisy' to the 'Old Rivingtonians' Association', whose motto 'Fostering friendships and nurturing nostalgia' lives itself out in genuine, caring friendships. My years at Rivington and Blackrod Grammar School were 1953 – 1960. We had great teachers and a wonderful headmaster, Mr Alan Jenner. I offer my thanks to every one of them.

I also dedicate this book to the Horwich Railway Mechanics' Institute Harriers whose club members still enjoy the annual Pike Fell Race; and to my maternal Grandfather, James Ridings (1875 – 1952), a boiler-maker at Horwich Locomotive Works and in whose memory a silver cup is competed for each Easter by the Junior Club members.

Chapter 1

'I'M REET SORRY, Miss Rossall but I can't offer yer a job.' The woman shrugged apologetically. 'Not wi' yer havin' the child, yer un'erstands.'

The door was shut in her face and Bea turned away. Yes, she did understand. She'd heard the same excuse before, countless times. How many days had she been trudging the streets from one establishment to another? Six? Seven? She'd lost count.

The cold wind and sleeting rain didn't help. It was fortunate she had been able to leave Daisy with Mrs Hurst, her housekeeper, or there would be two of them soaking wet. She fumbled in her pocket for her handkerchief and her frozen fingers encountered the letter she had received a few days ago. Her lips tightened as she pulled it out, a frown marring her face. Was this to be her only option? She had no need to read it again to remember what was written; the note was terse and concise.

Miss Rossall, I am aware of your current predicament. If you care to call at my house after 8:00 p.m. I have a proposition to put to you. Cyril Ackroyd.

Bea compressed her lips. The man was on the parish church council of her dear departed papa's church. She knew him – but didn't particularly like him. He was the owner of Ackroyd's spin-ning-mill and was renowned for being a ruthless taskmaster. He tolerated neither lateness nor absence and any dispute brought instant dismissal, forcing many a family into the workhouse.

So, what might his proposition be? Since the death of his wife almost two years ago, worn out by constant child-bearing, his two surviving sons had been packed off to a boarding school, so it wasn't her teaching skills that he had in mind. More than likely his latest housekeeper had given notice – or simply walked out – and he was in need of a replacement. Could she bear it? She hated the way his eyes raked over her – and the touch of his fingers made her flesh recoil. Fingers that stroked her hand when she handed him a hymn-book or slid up her inner wrist if she had been unable to avoid his departing handshake.

But did she have any other option? She glanced down at the sodden envelope again. The reality of the past few days was telling her, 'no'. She had to admit she was disappointed that none of their parishioners had felt able to help her in any way. Had none of them any compassion towards her? It seemed not.

At precisely eight o'clock that evening Bea knocked on the front door of Mr Ackroyd's house and eventually heard the sounds of the bolts being withdrawn and the grating of a key in the lock. She almost turned tail and ran – but what would it gain? She forced herself to stand her ground and face the mill-owner with cool reserve.

It was Mr Ackroyd himself who stood framed in the partly opened doorway. She supposed he was in his late forties, but his bewhiskered, angular face made him look older. His expres-sion darkened. 'In future, Miss Rossall, kindly remember that I expect my employees to use the side door, not the front one.'

'Good evening, Mr Ackroyd.' Bea greeted him in level tones, refusing to be cowed by him. 'I was not aware that I *am* an employee of yours. I have come in response to your note.'

'You took your time, miss!'

His tone was frosty but, strangely, that made Bea feel more confident.

'Yes. I am a busy person, Mr Ackroyd.'

'Busy traipsing the streets looking for employment, I hear,' he sneered. ''Ave yer been successful?'

His tone made Bea realize that he knew she hadn't. Had he had her followed? 'Nothing definite,' she prevaricated, thankful that there were one or two other options that she might investigate. 'I wondered what you had in mind by "a proposition"?'

He smiled thinly. 'I thought you might. You'd better step inside.' He moved back, opening the door a little wider and, with some trepidation, Bea stepped over the threshold and swept past him. It wasn't the first time she had entered the house. She had visited a number of times when Mrs Ackroyd was 'lying-in' after her several miscarriages and still-births. She strode firmly towards the front parlour and stepped inside.

A fire was burning in the hearth, with two armchairs pulled close beside it. Bea seated herself on the one at the far side of the hearth. Somehow, she felt safer sitting down. It put her into the category of 'visitor' instead of a potential employee attending an interview. Not that she felt relaxed. On the contrary, she perched herself stiffly upon its outer edge, her hands folded in her lap, hoping that the pose concealed the fact that her limbs were shaking.

She looked up at Mr Ackroyd, her expression one of pleasant enquiry, but she spoke no word. Let Mr Ackroyd be the one to lay his cards upon the table.

He made no move to seat himself. Bea could tell that her

refusal to act in a servile manner angered him, but before she had time to decide whether or not to soften her manner a little he was towering over her. 'I'll come straight to the point, Miss Rossall. I know that tha's in somewhat of a predicament and, although it's of your own makin', I'm willin', out of Christian charity, tha understands, to overlook it. Once tha's installed 'ere, I'll make sure that the rumour-mongers are dealt with.'

'Installed?' Bea queried, taken aback by his declaration. 'In what capacity? Your housekeeper? I presume Mrs Blackstock has left.'

'Call it what yer will. A man 'as needs – and needs a woman to fulfil 'em. Yer're no innocent maid, so I needn't mince my words. It's no wonder tha father died so sudden. It were probably out o' shame.'

Bea felt the blood drain from her face and then, just as quickly, flood it again. 'My father died of lung consumption,' she declared, her voice shaking, her mind still grappling with the rest of his words. 'You … you expect me to come and live here as a … a kept woman? How dare you insult me so?'

She began to rise from the chair but Mr Ackroyd pushed her down again. 'As I said, call it what yer will. Some would call yer a slut from the gutter. And yer needn't try to look offended by me words. Yer've a babby back at the vicarage to prove it. An' what yer'll do fer some slip of a lad in a back alley, yer'll do fer me in the comfort o' me own 'ome! An' yer'll do it right now! Try before yer buy is my motto!'

Terrified, Bea shrank back against the chair but he followed her down and bodily fell upon her, his mouth slobbering over hers as his hands probed and squeezed through the thickness of her coat, yanking at the buttons in his attempt to get it out of his way.

Bea had never been attacked in such a way and her actions

were purely instinctive. As Ackroyd partly lifted the weight of his body away from Bea in an attempt to pull away her clothing, Bea's arms were released from his weight and she swiftly clawed at the only part of him that was within reach – his face. Her nails weren't long, but they were strong and they left deep red gouges down both cheeks.

At the same time, pushing her left foot firmly against the floor as a lever, she jerked her right knee convulsively upwards in an attempt to kick him. Her knee was between his legs and slammed up against his body with considerable force. She didn't know the effect such an action would have upon a man but she saw its result. His body arched with pain and he toppled over on to the floor, both his hands now clutching between his legs.

Bea scrambled out of the chair and ran to the door. She glanced back, to make sure that he wasn't about to follow her. He was struggling to get to his feet, his face still twisted in pain.

'This ain't th'end of it!' he snarled, unable to regain his footing. 'I'll 'ave yer! Nobody else'll tek you on! Tha'll come crawling to me in the end! But get rid o' that bastard babby o' your'n afore tha does!'

Bea didn't wait to hear any more. She knew he was in no condition to follow her but, even so, she wasn't going to linger. She ran into the hall and out through the front door, slamming it shut behind her. Then, head down against the rain, she hurried back to the sanctuary of her home to sob out her story on to Mrs Hurst's motherly shoulder.

Beatrice hardly slept. Her thoughts raged back and forth, as she wondered how she might have handled it differently. Had she innocently led Mr Ackroyd to believe she might welcome his attentions? She didn't think so. He repelled her too much for that to have happened. But what was she to do next? She would never find employment with Ackroyd's hand against her!

Sleep must have overtaken her at some point but it was still dark when she awakened. She lay still for a moment, until the total silence in the room alerted her senses that something was different. She sat up in bed and listened intently.

Daisy! Where was Daisy? She had dreamed that Daisy was missing and she had been stumbling through darkened streets trying to find her. In a panic, she swung her legs out of bed and rushed to the door, grabbing hold of her dressing-gown from the end of her bed. She struggled into it as she crossed the small landing.

'Mrs Hurst? Where's Daisy?'

She could hear sounds from the kitchen – comforting, normal sounds of fire-irons against the range. As she stumbled down the stairs she heard Mrs Hurst's voice murmuring words that could only be being spoken to a baby, and she felt her panic subside. Daisy was safe. It had all been a nightmare.

No, not quite all of it! Not the part Mr Ackroyd had played. That had been real. And there would be repercussions, of that she was sure. She had innocently thought she could stay here, in this place where she had lived all her life, among the people she had grown up with. But now she knew she couldn't. She'd have to go away.

Bea found solace in tending to Daisy. The daily routine that had been thrust upon her last November, wreaking havoc with her parochial duties, had brought her through the recent dark days since her papa's death – and now it eased the distress she had experienced the previous evening at the hand of Cyril

Ackroyd. Holding Daisy against her shoulder, she stared blankly through the window into the vicarage's small garden. It wasn't a pretty garden, though her mama, God rest her soul, had always managed to coax some hardy flowers to keep on growing in spite of the soot-and-smoke-laden air from Salford's many factory chimneys. She swayed from side to side as she patted the tiny back with unaccustomed absent-mindedness. They were now more than halfway through March. The snowdrops were past their best and soon daffodil shoots would be pushing their way through the tired soil, eager to burst into flower.

A tiny burp near to Bea's ear drew a momentary response. 'Good girl!' she murmured soothingly. 'Let's see if you want the rest of your milk.' She sat down again on the wooden rocking-chair by the meagre fire and teased the tiny rosebud mouth open with the rubber teat, smiling with satisfaction when Daisy began to suck lustily once more.

Bea settled back against the cushion, allowing her thoughts to drift again, marvelling that Daisy, so tiny that she was thought to be about two months premature, had tenaciously held on to the thin thread of life instead of joining her young mother, buried in the churchyard. Now she was thriving and sleeping four hours between feeds – which was just as well, Bea thought grimly, since Daisy's future was as uncertain as her own.

'So, what yer gonna do, Miss Beatrice?' Mrs Hurst asked, pausing in her task of peeling some potatoes to put in the pan simmering over the fire. 'The new vicar'll be 'ere within a week. I know 'e said as 'ow yer could stay on fer a couple o' days until 'is family arrives, but it's only puttin' off the evil day, especially after what 'appened last neet! Eh, I wish I could tek yer wi' me to me sister's, but she's 'ard pressed to find room fer me, let alone you and the babby. Tha poor father'll be turnin' in 'is grave! 'Im as was as good a soul as ever lived! Yer've only to think 'ow 'e let yer take in young Elsie when 'er own folks disowned 'er! An' now what's going' ter 'appen to 'er babby and you, miss? That's what I'd like ter know!'

Beatrice rested her eyes on Daisy's contented face for a moment before she gave reply. She found it fascinating to watch the different expressions that flickered across the baby's face – eyebrows puckering as if in deep thought; tiny rosebud lips pursing as if in disapproval; a fleeting smile whispering across her small face. Oh, but what joy she had brought to this twice-bereaved household.

Tiny crystal teardrops glistened in Bea's eyes. She blinked them away and fumbled in her pocket for her handkerchief. 'I miss Papa, Mrs Hurst. How will I manage without his wise counsel?'

'Eh, I know, Miss Bea. 'E were a good man. His whole parish misses 'im. But think on what he taught you, an' always do what you know to be right. When your mama died, he felt lost fer a while but he always said he learned to lean more on his Saviour – and that's what got 'im through. That's what'll get you through as well!'

Bea nodded. Her lips compressed together as she was forced once more to confront her precarious future. How dare Mr Ackroyd treat her so! 'He thinks Daisy is mine,' she murmured aloud, with incredulity in her voice. 'Is that what everyone else thinks? Is that why no one will employ me? Surely I never looked as though I was with child?'

'What with your papa bein' so ill and you lookin' after Elsie as well, I don't suppose tha went out much, Miss Bea,' Mrs Hurst suggested. ''An' with it being winter, tha'd always got tha coat on. Folk'll always put two and two together and make five, especially if someone like Mr Ackroyd makes it 'is business to drop a hint here and there.'

'And Elsie begged us not to tell people about her expecting a baby,' Bea agreed. 'She hoped her parents would take her back once the baby was born – but all they wanted was her body for burial. They left Daisy with us. It never occurred to me that people would think she is mine. Even so, I can't bring myself to abandon her to the workhouse. But it seems I cannot get a job whilst I have her in my care.'

It wasn't as if she were asking for charity. She was intelligent; she could work hard. Hadn't she helped Mrs Hurst look after the vicarage and her dear papa since she was ten years old? A fact that hadn't escaped Cyril Ackroyd's notice. But he'd wanted both sides of his bread buttered – and with no thought of marriage in mind. Not that she had wanted such! Not with him! And he'd said she had to get rid of Daisy! The very thought tore at her heart. No, Cyril Ackroyd's way out of her predicament had had no appeal whatsoever.

Her other possibility of employment lay in the fact that she had taught a small group of ragged children their numbers and letters for a few hours every day in the vicarage's front parlour, and had managed to place some of them on the first rung of the ladder of employment. A ladder on which she was now finding it impossible to get a foothold. What she needed was a position as schoolmistress, with a small house attached or a room near by that she could rent.

But first she must resolve the problem of Daisy! That wasn't going to be easy, but she would not abandon the baby. She had promised Elsie.

She straightened her shoulders and took a deep breath. 'I'll have to do what we talked about the other day,' she said decisively. 'I will go to Horwich and try to find Mr Dearden. That is where the newspaper cutting that Elsie had says he lives. *"Mr Henry Dearden of Endmoor House,"'* she quoted from memory. 'That sounds as though he is a gentleman, does it not? Well, if he is as fine a gentleman as Elsie would have had us believe, surely he will want to know of the existence of his small daughter and take on the responsibility of rearing her? Even if he is unable to recognize her openly, surely he will know of some kind lady who would rear her as one of her own, for some kind of recompense?'

Being more worldly wise than the late vicar's daughter, Mrs Hurst sniffed. 'The gentry don't always do as they ought, Miss Bea. 'E'd no right ter tek advantage o' such a young girl as Elsie Brindle, swearin' he loved 'er and promisin' ter marry 'er! And what was 'er employer thinkin' of, casting 'er off like that, when she ought ter 'ave taken more care of 'er female staff? It's a wicked world, Miss Bea, that's what it is!'

'Yes, but we've got to believe in the goodness of man, too,' Bea persisted. 'Papa always used to say that goodness is there, if only you look hard enough!'

'Hmm! Well, 'e was a saint and no mistake!' Mrs Hurst commented. 'And this Mr Dearden just as surely isn't! But let's 'ope 'e 'as some form of conscience! Now, yer've got that bit o' money from sellin' most of yer poor father's books and yer bits o' furniture; so use a bit of it to put up in an 'otel fer the night and see if yer can find someone to mind Daisy fer yer when yer goes to see 'im. Yer'll be able to weigh up the situation better that way.'

'Yes,' Bea agreed, adding with a sigh, 'Though how I shall face up to handing Daisy over to a stranger, I just don't know. I'm not looking forward to confronting Mr Dearden with the result of his dalliance – but I *am* hoping he will be prepared to provide for Daisy's upkeep and care.'

Chapter 2

F RIDAY WAS OVERCAST, the clouds holding in the pall of smoke from the factory chimneys, making the air thick, damp and cold. Bea hadn't been out of the house since Mr Ackroyd's attack upon her. It had shaken her more than she had at first thought and she had given in to Mrs Hurst's pleas that she 'take it easy fer a day or two'. A discreet enquiry made by Mrs Hurst to one of their neighbours elicited the information that Mr Ackroyd had not put in an appearance at his mill either.

'Good!' was Bea's uncharitable greeting to this news. 'I hope his face is marred evermore, like the mark of Cain!'

''Andsome, 'e never was,' Mrs Hurst stated dourly, 'but 'e won't be none too 'appy over explainin' them scratches. We needs to get you out of 'is way afore 'e comes lookin' fer yer.'

Consequently, on Friday morning Bea, dressed in her workday frock, put on her black woollen coat that had been hanging on the wooden rack over the kitchen fire since its soaking on Tuesday evening. A serviceable bonnet covered her dark-chestnut hair, now drawn back into an unflattering bun which, along with a pair of her papa's reading-glasses, Bea had devised as a means to deter any untoward passion from any prospective employers she might encounter over the next few days; her gloves, discreetly darned in a number of places, kept the bitter cold from her fingers.

Daisy was cocooned in a shawl, the ends of which Bea had tied around herself to act as a sort of sling, allowing her to support Daisy's weight with her left arm and also carry a small cloth bag dangling from its straps. Also wrapped within the shawl, between her own and Daisy's bodies, was a bottle of heated milk. Its heat would help to keep Daisy warm and keep some of its own warmth for Daisy's next feed.

The bag contained another bottle of milk; a change of towelling nappies; two slices of thickly cut bread with a thin slice of boiled bacon placed between for her midday meal; a letter of character reference from the doctor who had tended both her parents and herself; and her purse. In her right hand she held an ancient valise, containing some baby clothes and a few items of clothing for herself; her parents' marriage certificate and her own birth certificate; her bank book containing a few pounds; and a few small mementoes. As Bea trekked to Salford railway station, both the valise and Daisy seemed to grow heavier by the minute.

The station teemed with the hustle and bustle of many would-be travellers. Bea stood still, momentarily bewildered by the grandness of the iron-structured building with its high glass roof and the noises that reverberated under its canopy. Trains were arriving and departing with the gushing sound of steam; railway employees were shouting instructions; and strident whistles blew as trains were deemed ready to depart; and the air was filled with the general hubbub of numerous travellers.

Manchester was the cotton centre of northern England. Its cotton exchange was the very hub of the city's financiers, and cotton mills abounded, spewing black smoke out of the tall factory chimneys, their furnaces gobbling up the coal that was delivered to the premises along the network of canals from the

surrounding mining towns. Nowadays, the new-fangled railways were criss-crossing the landscape, carrying goods even
more speedily, and railway towns were springing up every-
where. It was a time of growth; a time to be looking forward.

It was the need for growth that had taken surveyors of the
Lancashire and Yorkshire Railway Company at Miles Platting,
now hemmed in by the sprawling outer environs of northern
Manchester, to seek a new site upon which to expand their
workshops. In 1884 they had settled on Horwich, a small town
to the west of Bolton. Here, new workshops had been
constructed and were now in non-stop production, keeping the
designers and draughtsmen busy in their offices and
designing-rooms.

Bea had learned, simply and fortuitously by conversing with
one of the 'interregnum' preachers sent by the bishop to fulfil
her dying papa's duties, that Mr Henry Dearden – the man
mentioned in Elsie's newspaper cutting – was one of these
designers. She knew nothing else about him, except that he
lived in Horwich. She had hoped to have time to make further
enquiries, but Cyril Ackroyd's attack upon her had taken away
that option. Now she must confront him with little more than
circumstantial evidence – and the good word of an honest, and
wronged, maidservant. She hoped it would be enough!

But now, in the hustle and bustle of this busy railway
station, her courage dwindled a little. She had never before
travelled on one of the iron monsters that belched out steam
and sooty smoke into the already smoke-laden air of Salford –
though she had heard them and had felt the ground beneath
her feet shake as they rumbled over the viaduct that spanned
the road in the middle of her father's parish. But this was a
different noise. It went on and on until her head seemed to be
buzzing with it, making her feel light-headed and dizzy. The

unfamiliar spectacles probably accounted for part of that, she realized, but she was loath to take them off. The more prim and plain she appeared, the safer she would feel. Fortunately her papa's eyes had been very good for his age and the lenses were quite weak. Even so, people seemed to be a little out of focus and she found it more beneficial to peer over the top of the rims, unconsciously mimicking a subterfuge her papa had often resorted to.

Her ticket purchased, she then had to find the right platform, juggling Daisy and her luggage in order to show her ticket to the official at the turnstile, before hurrying alongside the third-class carriages, looking anxiously into each compartment until she found one with some seats still free. A middle-aged man courteously offered to place her valise on to the rack above their heads. She didn't correct him when he addressed her as 'missus'. She had no need to explain her circumstances to strangers – and certainly not that the train fare had taken a good part of her small amount of money in her purse.

She was thankful to be able to sink on to the hard wooden seat and get her breath back. Her mind teemed with endless thoughts. Was she doing the right thing? How would Mr Dearden respond? What if he refused to listen? Or simply disbelieved her? But what alternative did she have? She had no wish to face Mr Ackroyd again. Her face flamed at the memory of what he had done. She shuddered. She felt defiled. He had taken her by surprise. The touch of his hands and his mouth had repelled her.

No, it was best that she left the area and made a new start. She *must* find a means of earning her living. The small amount of money she had wouldn't last long. However painful parting from Daisy would no doubt prove to be, there was no other way.

Together, they would starve. With Daisy being taken care of, Bea would stand a better chance of obtaining some form of employment. Maybe in Horwich itself? Surely that would be far enough away from Cyril Ackroyd? He would have no idea where she had gone. Mrs Hurst was the only person who knew of her plans and she would never disclose that information. Once she was removed from his reach he would forget all about her – as she now determined to forget all about him.

Doors slammed; a whistle blew; a loud burst of steam belched from the engine and billowed past the window – and the train jerked into motion. Bea set her thoughts ahead. Horwich was where her future lay. It was a rapidly expanding industrial town, nestling against the tumbling ends of the Pennines. Surely, such a town would hold many opportunities for someone such as herself? And, if heaven smiled upon her, she nurtured the hope that she would be able to keep some form of contact with Daisy. It was that thought that buoyed her spirit as the train rumbled its way between tall dark buildings, past factories and the ends of terraced housing whose décor would forever bear the dark sooty grains that became part of the air the city-dwellers breathed.

As the train drew into Bolton station Bea belatedly remembered being told that she would have to change to another train here, a local connection to Horwich. This fact was borne out by a porter's voice proclaiming, 'Change 'ere fer 'Orwich! Change 'ere fer 'Orwich!'

'Oh, my goodness!' Bea exclaimed. She jumped to her feet, straight away falling sideways on to the lap of a man sitting on the opposite side of the compartment as the train lurched to a standstill. Daisy let out a yell as she was jolted out of her slumber.

'Oh, I'm sorry! Please forgive me!' Bea stammered. 'I didn't realize! Oh, thank you!' as willing hands reached out to help her to her feet. She stood, swaying unsteadily, disorientated by her fall. She awkwardly pushed her spectacles more firmly on to her nose.

Everyone in the compartment had risen to their feet in consternation. Bea felt overpowered by their close proximity. Daisy, unused to being in such a crush of people, began to cry lustily as a porter flung open the door.

'Change 'ere fer 'Orwich!'

'Come on, missus! Let's get you out of this crush!' the man who had lifted up her valise said loudly, encouraging those nearer the door either to sit down again, or else make their own way out of the carriage. 'I'll get yer bag down, don't worry, missus,' he assured her.

'Thank you!' Bea gasped gratefully, accepting the assistance of a buxom middle-aged woman who was supporting her by her right elbow as she edged towards the door. Someone else steadied the arm holding Daisy as she carefully stepped down the steep step to the platform. 'Oh, thank you all,' she said again, feeling quite embarrassed by being the centre of attention. 'You're all so kind. I'm all right, now. Really, I am.'

'Come and sit down over 'ere in the waitin' room,' the buxom woman urged her. 'Tha'll feel much better in a few minutes.'

'But I need to get the train to Horwich,' Bea protested.

'Eh, that's all reet. It don't go fer another five minutes. Let's get that babby settled. She's reet upset.'

'Yes, you're right,' Bea agreed, allowing herself to be ushered into the waiting room. 'Maybe I should give her some milk? That would settle her.' She crossed over to the benchlike seats and sat Daisy down. She undid her shawl. 'See, her bottle is here. It's still quite warm. Come on, my little love, it's milky time.'

'I'll go an' see if the train's ready,' her helper offered. 'Tha could carry on wi' the bottle on the train, couldn't yer?'

'Yes – and maybe change her as well, if there's room in the carriage. I've got a spare nappy here in my bag,' Bea agreed, glancing casually to where her cloth bag should have been dangling from her left arm – but it wasn't there!

'My bag's gone!' Bea exclaimed in disbelief, staring with wide eyes at the woman. 'It's gone!' She leaped up from the seat, her movement abruptly pulling the teat of the bottle out of Daisy's mouth. Daisy protested loudly. Bea felt torn between her concern about her missing bag and Daisy's loud objections to the cessation of her feed. 'My bag's gone! What shall I do?'

'Isn't that yer bag?' the woman asked, pointing to her valise that had been placed on the bench near the door by the helpful man from their carriage.

'Yes – but I had another one. A cloth one. It was hanging from my arm. Maybe I dropped it?' She snatched up Daisy and hurried out on to the platform. The train had gone on its way to Chorley and then Preston but there were a number of people standing in small groups, probably waiting for other trains. There was no sign of her bag on the ground. Further on, a few passengers were still straggling towards the steep steps that led to the exit. A porter was following behind them, pushing a trolley loaded with a number of bags but none looked like her small cloth bag. Another porter, probably the one who had opened the carriage doors, was ambling along towards an office.

'Excuse me! Please wait!' Bea called, hurrying after the porter, patting Daisy's back as she held her against her shoulder. 'I've lost my bag! Has anyone handed it in? It's a cloth one. Black. It has long handles. It was over my arm!' She knew she was babbling but all her money was in it, and Daisy's other bottle, and some clean nappies: everything she needed for the journey.

The man turned round. 'Nowt's been handed in, missus. Where did yer last see it?'

'In the train compartment – the one from Salford. I stumbled as the train stopped. Everyone was crushed around me. I was holding the baby. I couldn't have dropped it. It was on my arm.' Bea felt frantic. How was she to continue her journey? If her bag was gone, so was her money – and she didn't know where to find a bank where she could withdraw any of her meagre savings. And, even if she did find one, it would be closed before she could get there. And her ticket for the rest of the journey was in the bag! That had gone, too. She looked around, hoping to see it lying forlornly on the ground, even trampled underfoot – but it wasn't there.

The shrill hooter of a train at a platform across the lines from where was she standing rent the air, reminding her that she needed to continue with her journey.

'Is that the train to Horwich? It's my connection! I need to get on it!' She took a step towards a bridge that crossed the lines – then stopped. Her valise! She whirled round towards the waiting room – but stopped again. She'd no ticket! And, without her purse, no means of paying for one.

'Tha'll 'ave ter come to the station-master's office an' fill in a form,' the porter cut into her befuddled mind.

'A form?' she repeated blankly.

'A "missin' baggage" form,' the porter explained patiently. 'In case yer bag turns up somewhere – though I doubt it. It's probably been stolen.'

Beatrice reluctantly feared the same. With her holding Daisy as she had been doing, the bag could only have been taken if someone had cut through its cloth handles. 'Then what can I do? My ticket's been stolen, too, and I need to get to Horwich.'

'Come an' see the stationmaster. 'E'll sort thee out. Tha can get the next train in a couple of 'ours or so. Come on. Th'office is this way.'

'I need to get my valise. It's all I've got.'

The porter called instructions about its retrieval to another porter who was now passing by with an empty trolley, then he led Bea and the still-wailing Daisy into the stationmaster's office, where he passed on the details of Beatrice's problems to the stationmaster himself.

'Right, missus. Now, where's them forms?'

As the stationmaster rummaged in a number of drawers to find the appropriate form, Bea patted Daisy's back soothingly, trying to calm herself at the same time. She heard the whistle shrill from the guard of the train at the other platform, followed by a burst of steam and a clanking shunt as the engine's pistons strained to set the iron monster in motion.

Her heart sank. Even if she were allowed to travel on to Horwich today, she would be arriving much later than she had planned – and, with her money gone, she had no means of delaying her confrontation with Mr Dearden until the following day. She would have to visit him as soon as she arrived in Horwich – with Daisy in her arms!

Chapter 3

IT WAS MID-AFTERNOON when the connecting train from Bolton to Horwich departed from Bolton station, more than two anxious hours later than Bea had intended, and she was now desperate to reach her destination. The shock of losing her bag weighed heavily upon her but, as she stared through the dirty window of the train, she gradually became aware of green fields and small coppices and an occasional isolated group of farm buildings. She absent-mindedly removed her spectacles so that she could see more clearly; she hadn't realized that so much open countryside lay within half a day's journey from the city centre. Why, even in this dismal weather it looked lovely: so green! She laughed – of course it was green. Grass usually was.

From her early childhood, she had been encouraged to count her blessings instead of listing her woes and now, restored by the sight of God's wonderful countryside, she reflected that at least Daisy had been fed and was once more happily asleep and cocooned in the warm shawl and the stationmaster had provided a replacement ticket for her to show to the ticket collector. Surely, there was still hope for a favourable outcome of her journey.

After a steep curve of the railway line, more buildings came into view and Bea suspected that they were almost at their journey's end. The air wasn't quite as smoke-laden as in the city but the low clouds, hanging over them like a thick, dirty blanket, seemed almost to touch the chimney-tops.

As the train eventually hissed to a halt, Bea replaced her spectacles and hugged Daisy against her chest. This time she remained seated until one of the other passengers in her compartment had pulled on the strap to let down the window so that he could grasp the door handle on the outside to open the door. She didn't want another tumble.

"Orwich Station! All change!' called a porter, making his way along the platform and opening the doors as he passed. Another male passenger lifted down her valise. Bea almost snatched it from him but common sense prevailed and she let him carry it on to the platform for her.

"Ere y'are, missus,' he said, holding out his other hand to assist her as she stepped down. 'Don't want tha dropping that babby.'

'Thank you.' She paused a little forlornly as he and other passengers confidently made their way towards the exit. She had arrived in Horwich but she had no idea in which direction to proceed. And time was rushing on. She had much to do before the day was over.

She followed the others to the ticket-collector at the exit, her ticket held awkwardly in the hand supporting Daisy. As the ticket collector took it from her, she asked hesitantly, 'I ... I wonder if you can help me? It's my first time here and I'm not sure how to get to my destination. I am ... er ... visiting a Mr Dearden who lives at Endmoor House.'

He pushed back his cap and looked at her curiously. 'Aye, that's where Mr Dearden lives.'

Bea realized that the sight of her with a young baby in her arms, asking directions to the house of a locally-known man, must inevitably cause some speculation, but she couldn't allow that to deter her from her purpose. She tilted up her chin. 'Can you tell me how to reach his home?'

'Aye, it's up the road past the church. But t'is a fair walk wi' a babby to carry, missus. D'yer want me ter call a cab fer yer?'

Bea shook her head. She couldn't afford such a luxury. 'No, thank you. I'm sure I will manage it.'

The porter looked doubtful. 'If tha says so. Reet! Well, as I said, tha goes up ter the top o' this road and turn right, on to Church Street. Go on up past the parish church and tha'll come to Endmoor 'Ouse on the left just before th'old stocks. Yer can't miss it. It's a big 'ouse, set back from the road. Tha'd best get a move on, mind. The heavens are about to open. It's been threatenin' all day!'

Bea glanced upward apprehensively. The clouds had thickened in the past few minutes and were now quite black. Oh dear! That was all she needed.

'Thank you. You've been most helpful.'

As Bea turned away huge raindrops began to fall, making large wet splashes on the ground. Within minutes the rain was bouncing up off the cobbled roadway. Bea strode out as strongly as she was able, her heart sinking as she saw that the gradient became steeper on Church Street. Long before she had reached the parish church, her coat was soaked, the cold wetness seeping through to her skin. Rainwater dripped from the brim of her bonnet and ran down her face, making her spectacles almost opaque with the rivulets of water. She bent her head against the flow and pressed on, her feet squelching with every step. Daisy began to whimper.

'It's not much further, darling,' Bea whispered, more for her own benefit than Daisy's. How would she be received? What would she do if she were turned away?

She paused as she drew level with the vicarage. Should she go there to seek shelter? She knew that her father would have taken pity on any traveller caught in such inclement weather – as indeed Elsie Brindle had gratefully discovered last October. That memory reminded Bea of the delicate nature of her purpose in making the journey. She doubted Mr Dearden would welcome any rumours of his ungentlemanly conduct towards Elsie being mooted abroad among his neighbours, and if she were to throw herself on the mercy of the local vicar, that would inevitably be the outcome. No, she must proceed to Endmoor House as planned and trust that Mr Dearden's response would be an honourable one, however belated it might be.

Head down against the rain, she trudged on, her face stinging with the icy onslaught. Her mind seemed to be enveloped by an unreal aura of confusion that made her want to sink down on to the ground and let oblivion wipe away the utter weariness that had overtaken her. A thin thread of common sense made her keep moving. Then, just when she felt she couldn't go a step further, she saw the words, **Endmoor House**, carved in the stone pillars of a gateway. She'd arrived.

The house seemed to loom towards her through the persistent downpour. Its dark bulk was intimidating. She hugged Daisy more tightly and went up the path towards the front entrance. A flight of four wide steps led to the door, which was set between two stone pillars. Bay windows jutted out on both sides of the doorway, bays that continued up to the upper floor. Heavy curtains hung at the windows but no flare of light glowed through.

She paused at the foot of the short flight of steps, conscious of her bedraggled state. It hardly seemed fitting to expect to be admitted by the front door. She turned to her right and followed the path around the side of the house. Here, a light was streaming from a downstairs window, casting a glow into the garden. Although the curtains were still drawn back, the windowsill was too high for her to peep inside as she passed by. Ahead was a wooden gate, fortunately unlocked. Beyond it a number of outbuildings were grouped around a square cobbled yard. At the far side, a low gate showed that a garden of some sort stretched out behind the house, but the falling curtain of rain made its size and contents indistinct. Bea swung her glance back to the side of the house where two steps led up to a solid wooden door.

She closed her eyes and whispered a short prayer for strength before mounting the steps and rapping upon the door. A few moments passed and Bea could imagine whoever was within wondering what sort of visitor could be out on such a day as this. Eventually she heard the sound of the key being turned and her mind seemed to recoil, as the memory of waiting outside Cyril Ackroyd's house swept over her. No! She mustn't think of that! Besides, where could she run to from here? She *had* to persevere with her plan.

The door was pulled open to reveal the stout figure of a woman dressed in a black frock covered by a white apron. An appetizing aroma of freshly baked bread drifted out through the door, making Bea's mouth begin to water. She had had no lunch and the smell of food made her realize how hungry she was.

'Yes? What d'yer want?' the woman enquired abruptly. Her gaze dropped to the bundle in Bea's arm. 'We don't deal with no gypsies,' she declared. 'Nor do we buy at the door. Be off wi' yer!' She stepped back and began to close the door. Bea quickly thrust her elbow against the door.

'No! I'm not selling anything. I need to see Mr Dearden.'

The woman folded her arms across her bosom. 'Oh, aye? An' who are you to demand to see Mr Dearden?'

'I need ...'

Some noise from another part of the house drifted through a connecting door. It sounded like children laughing in a taunting way.

Bea wasn't sure how she felt about children being in the house. It made Mr Dearden a family man – with added complications in the form of a wife – who might prefer to ignore the existence of an illegitimate child. Oh dear, she was sure Elsie hadn't known he was married.

The woman glanced towards the sound, making a tutting sound and rolling her eyes in a scornful manner. She looked back at Bea – and Bea was surprised to see a gleam of satisfaction in her eyes. She sensed that whoever was causing the rumpus was doing so with this woman's tacit approval.

Before she could think any further, the door at the opposite side of the kitchen was flung open and a man's voice demanded, 'What the devil is going on upstairs, Mrs Kellett?'

'I'm sure I don't know, Mr Dearden!' Mrs Kellett replied tartly. 'Miss Winstanley makes it quite plain that she wants no interference from me! And, besides, why isn't Nanny Adams seeing to it? Surely she can 'ear it!'

So this was Mr Dearden, Bea mused, only half-listening to the conversation between the two. She felt quite light-headed, almost as if she were a spectator viewing the whole scene from outside herself. The man was tall and slender, his face at present marred by an angry expression. He seemed a little older than she had expected him to be – maybe in his mid-thirties? Though why she had assumed him to be younger she wasn't sure. She couldn't remember Elsie mentioning his age. Just that she had called him a 'young gentleman'. Whatever his age, he had acted extremely irresponsibly! The more so, if he were married with children. What would his wife think when confronted with an illegitimate baby? Would she insist that he should send Bea away?

Bea's courage almost failed her, but she found herself bristling again when he impatiently replied, 'I don't *know* why Nanny Adams isn't dealing with it. All I know is I can't be doing with such a disturbance just now. I'm trying to get my work done. Will you go upstairs and see what's going on, Mrs Kellett?'

Mrs Kellett swung back to face Bea before doing as her master demanded. 'You'd best be off! As you can see, Mr Dearden's a busy man. He 'as no time to be dealing with the likes of you. An' you're letting all that nasty weather into my kitchen.'

She tried to shut the door but Bea stepped forward and put the weight of her body against it. This might be her only chance to speak to the man. She couldn't let it pass.

'I need to speak to you, Mr Dearden!' she called out. 'It's important!'

'We'll 'ave no impertinence from you!' Mrs Kellett asserted, thrusting her open palm against Bea's chest, making Bea stagger backwards. Fortunately, the doorjamb stopped Bea from falling down the steps but the jolting caused Daisy to let out a wail of distress.

'What's going on?' Mr Dearden demanded.

'I'm just gettin' rid of this … person, sir. She's got no business—'

'But I *do* have business with Mr Dearden!' Bea insisted desperately. She couldn't bear to be thrust out into the rain again – not before she had confronted this man with his responsibility towards Daisy. 'Please spare me a few minutes, Mr Dearden.'

Another loud shriek of laughter sounded from somewhere in the house, causing Mr Dearden to say sharply, 'Go and see what it's all about, Mrs Kellett. I'll deal with this.' He held open the inner door, his face set as Mrs Kellett threw a backward glance at Bea before stalking past him, mumbling some words that Bea didn't catch.

'Thank you, Mrs Kellett,' Mr Dearden murmured, his eyes flicking upwards in a show of long-suffering patience. 'Right, young lady, what is it you want to speak to me about?' Before Bea had the chance to reply, he gestured impatiently. 'Come inside – and shut the door! It's like a gale blowing in here. Come on, I haven't got all day.'

He paused as he took in Bea's appearance – looking as if he had only just seen her in any detail. 'You're soaking wet! And you've got a young baby with you. Are you begging? There's a relief centre in the Methodist church, you know. That's where you should go if you need help.'

He came a couple of steps nearer as Bea said quietly, 'I'm not begging.' Her body began to shake and she swayed slightly.

Mr Dearden moved quickly and reached out his hand to steady her. He took the valise out of her hand and drew her further into the kitchen. 'You'd better sit down, young lady. You're shivering. Whatever are you doing, being out in this weather with such a young baby? Gertie, bring one of those chairs here!'

Bea had barely registered that a young kitchen-maid was present, nor, now, that the girl did as her master asked. Her whole body began to shake uncontrollably. If Daisy hadn't been tied into her shawl, she would have dropped her. She allowed Mr Dearden to guide her towards the chair and sank gratefully on to it, thankful that Daisy had been lulled back to sleep by the warmth of the kitchen.

Her spectacles had steamed up in the warmth of the kitchen and Bea awkwardly unhooked them off her ears with one hand. That was better. Her eyes immediately relaxed into their normal range of vision. She saw a flicker of interest in his eyes and she knew she must put them on again. She eased the ear-rests into a different place.

'Is that tea still hot, Gertie?' Mr Dearden asked, indicating a teapot with a knitted cosy over it.

Gertie touched the pot and nodded enthusiastically. 'Yes, sir. Shall I get 'er a cup, sir?'

'Yes, please. Would you like a cup of tea, Mrs...? Er ... I'm afraid I don't know your name.' He looked at her quizzically.

'It's Beatrice Rossall – *Miss* Beatrice Rossall,' she added, her eyes challenging him as she gave her unmarried status.

He merely glanced down at Daisy and raised an eyebrow, causing Bea's face to flush at the implication of the silent gesture.

'The baby is not mine!' she snapped.

'Really?' He shrugged, as he lifted the teapot and gestured it towards her. 'Tea?'

Bea would have loved to refuse – but her hunger and inner chill gnawed at her. 'Yes, please,' she said primly. 'Thank you.'

'Sugar?' He picked up the sugar-tongs and held them poised over the small basin.

'No thank you.' It was one luxury she had been forced to forgo over the past few weeks as her money dwindled away.

Mr Dearden overrode her answer. 'I think you'd better. I believe it to be of remedial value in times of distress.' He gener-ously dropped two lumps of sugar into the tea and stirred it briskly. 'Here, drink this. It will make you feel a bit warmer – and maybe you'd like one of Mrs Kellett's scones?' He removed two from the rack upon which a batch was cooling, split them with a knife and layered on some butter. 'I'll have one myself. They're quite delicious.'

He placed two halves on to a small plate and pushed it towards Bea, then perched on the edge of the table as he picked up a half-scone for himself. His glance rested upon her.

Beatrice felt uncomfortable under his gaze but was too hungry to care what he was thinking. She murmured her thanks and took a large bite of the scone. She couldn't stop herself from chewing it hastily and washing it down with a mouthful of hot tea. A second mouthful dispatched the rest of that half and she hesitated before picking up the other half. 'My lunch was stolen,' she offered by way of explanation. 'I am not usually so hasty in my manner of eating.'

Mr Dearden inclined his head slightly to indicate that he believed her. He took another scone from the cooling-rack, buttered it and put it on her plate. 'Have another, Miss Rossall – and then, when you have appeased your hunger, you may tell me why you are so determined to speak to me that you have risked this young baby's health, and your own, by coming here in today's appalling weather. I confess I find it extremely irresponsible of you!'

Beatrice had picked up another half of scone and it was halfway to her mouth when he spoke his censure of her. Her hand halted and she carefully replaced the scone on to her plate. She brushed the crumbs off her fingers and, for a brief moment, placed both hands around Daisy whilst she tried to compose herself.

She failed. She stood abruptly and faced him, swaying a little as she did so. She gripped hold of the edge of the table and summoned whatever strength remained within her. 'It is not *I* who have behaved irresponsibly, Mr Dearden! It is you! You, who took advantage of a poor, innocent maidservant and, after fathering a child, left her to her fate!'

The crash of a broken plate and a faintly muttered, 'Crikey!'

reminded her of the kitchen-maid's presence at the sink. The girl had swung round to stare at her, her eyes wide with a mixture of shock and excitement. Bea now felt ashamed of her outburst. She had practised ways of confronting Mr Dearden with the outcome of his dalliance but none of them had been quite so forceful – and not intended to be in anyone else's hearing. As remorse rose within her, she realized that Mr Dearden had put down his scone and had slowly levered himself off the edge of the table. He now stood towering above her, his face white with … what? Shock? Anger? She feared it was the latter and she took a step away from him. Surely he wasn't going to hit her! She knew that some men, men like Cyril Ackroyd, reacted violently in such situations but, for some reason, she hadn't expected it here.

But it was the kitchen-maid he spoke to, his voice cold but controlled.

'Gertie, go and see if Mrs Kellet needs any help, will you? Leave the broken plate. You can sweep it up later.'

Gertie scuttled out of the kitchen, her face agog with excitement and curiosity, no doubt ready to pour the tale into Mrs Kellet's ears.

Bea grimaced ruefully but made herself meet Mr Dearden's gaze. 'I'm sorry,' she apologized. 'I shouldn't have spoken in such a way in front of the kitchen-maid.'

'But you don't retract the accusation?' he levelled at her.

'No. Why should I, when it is true? A young girl's life was ruined. Whilst you came home to all of this …' She gestured around, before continuing with added heat and scorn in her voice, '… this comfort and warmth, Elsie was thrown out of her place of employment and had to make her way on foot into the middle of the city to her family, the ones whom she thought would give her support and comfort – only to be cast out once more because of the shame her condition would bring upon them. Shame caused by *your* irresponsible conduct, Mr Dearden. So, don't accuse *me* of irresponsibility. Look rather to yourself.'

Before Mr Dearden had time to respond, the inner kitchen door crashed open and a dishevelled woman of about forty years of age burst into the kitchen. Her angry face was streaked with paint, as were her hair and clothes.

'Just look what those fiends have done to me, Mr Dearden!' she screamed at him, as she advanced into kitchen. The bulk of the kitchen table halted her progress and she thrust her face forward across it. 'They are worse than wild heathens! They should be beaten and locked away! I am leaving, Mr Dearden! Do you hear? Leaving, this very minute!'

Chapter 4

BEA STARED AT the woman. What on earth had been happening upstairs? How many children were there in this strange household that they were able to terrify their governess? Was this incident typical of their behaviour? She was beginning to doubt the wisdom of her plan to have this man acknowledge Daisy as his child and leave her here to be brought up within his household.

She was momentarily distracted as Gertie sidled back into the kitchen in the irate woman's wake. The maid crept sideways round the edge of the room, her awed attention fixed on the scene being played out before her. When she reached the sink Gertie's sense of servitude recalled her to her task-in-hand. She swooped down under the sink, grabbed hold of a brush and dustpan and began to sweep the broken pieces of crockery into a neat pile.

Bea swung her gaze back to Mr Dearden, wondering how he was reacting to the second verbal attack upon him, following, as it did, so soon upon her own harsh accusation. However, his response surprised her.

'Come and sit down, Miss Winstanley,' he said quite calmly. He picked up the teapot again. 'Would you like a cup of tea?'

Bea almost laughed hysterically. Was a cup of tea his panacea for all life's ills?

'No, I would not!' Miss Winstanley cried at him. 'I have had enough of this mad household and those ...' She pressed her thin lips tightly together, seeming to be about to choke on the words she was holding back. '... those ... devil's spawn you harbour under your roof!'

Mr Dearden straightened his back. His cheeks seemed white with suppressed anger, but his expression was almost impassive. Only a slight twitch of a muscle under his right eye betrayed his fury. 'Miss Winstanley, sit down. I'm sure you will ...' he began in an attempt to pacify her, though the coldness of his tone portrayed no hint that he might be about to voice some sympathy.

In any case, the agitated woman was in no mood to be pacified. She held up her hand, palm forward across the table. 'No, Mr Dearden. I have had enough. Those monsters bound and gagged me in my chair and proceeded to dance around me like wild Indians, splattering me with paint and bombarding me with missiles!' Her voice rose to a shriek as she added, 'They threatened to scalp me! I will not stay one minute longer than I need to. I will leave immediately. Do you hear? Immediately!'

Bea was instinctively jogging the still-sleeping Daisy in her arms, hoping that the soothing motion would counteract the harsh tone of Miss Winstanley's voice. She had listened to the woman's diatribe in a state of dazed wonder but the governess's decision to leave immediately, jolted her alert. Did the woman not realize how atrocious the weather had become? She glanced swiftly at Mr Dearden in order to see his reaction.

He, too, seemed startled. 'I beg you not to act too hastily, Miss Winstanley. The hour is late and the weather most inclement. Perhaps by morning you may wish to reconsider your decision?'

Miss Winstanley took a deep breath and drew herself up to her full height. 'My decision is made, Mr Dearden,' she said more calmly. 'You will get a cab for me and book me in for an overnight stay at the Crown Hotel – at your expense, of course. I am going upstairs to pack my belongings. You will inform me when the cab arrives.' She whirled round and strode out of the kitchen and, presumably, up the stairs leaving a stunned silence behind her, a silence broken only by a whimper from Daisy.

Bea lifted the baby so that her lips were able to caress the little cheek, now feeling warm to her touch. She glanced once more at Mr Dearden.

The strange thing was, Mr Dearden hadn't seemed all that surprised by the unexpected incident. Angry at the words used to describe his children, yes … but surprised? No. Not even by the governess's determination to leave immediately. She was impressed by his impassive response.

However, when Mr Dearden at last turned to face her, Bea could see that he was far from being in complete control of his emotions. Nervously he adjusted his necktie and pulled at the cuffs of his sleeves, though they had been in no disorder as far as Bea could determine. He gave a slight cough.

'If you will excuse me, Miss … er … Rossall, it seems I must make urgent arrangements on behalf of Miss Winstanley.' He turned towards the kitchen-maid. 'Gertie, I am sorry but I am going to have to send you out in this appalling weather. Put on your coat and run down to the Gregsons's house. Ask Mr Gregson to send his son Johnny to Livesey's stables to order a cab to convey Miss Winstanley to the Crown Hotel as soon as is convenient. Have you got all that?'

Gertie bobbed a quick curtsey, her eyes wide … though whether with shock or excitement, Bea was unable to determine.

'Yessir,' the maid squeaked. She scurried round the kitchen table, took a shabby coat from a hook by the back door, hastily shrugged herself into it and pulled open the door. The squall of wind and rain invaded the warmth of the kitchen.

'Run straight there and back again,' Mr Dearden admonished as Gertie plunged outdoors.

Bea was surprised at the kindness of his tone. Mr Dearden did not appear to be the person she had imagined him to be. She had to remind herself forcibly that this man had ruined the life of a young servant and inadvertently caused her death ... and, more importantly, orphaned Daisy.

She realized that Mr Dearden was edging around the kitchen table towards the inner door. She mustn't let him disappear. 'Mr Dearden—'

He held out his hand, palm towards her. 'Miss ... er ... Rossall, as you can see, I must beg leave of you to postpone any further discussion concerning the other matter you raised so forcefully. Tomorrow, perhaps? Would that be convenient to you?'

In spite of understanding the delicate situation into which Mr Dearden had been thrust, the thought of having to go back outside into the pouring rain without having resolved the question of Daisy's future care was too much for Bea.

'No, tomorrow won't be convenient, Mr Dearden,' she said firmly. 'I have nowhere to stay overnight. My money was stolen and I am a stranger in this town.'

He stared blankly at her. 'What are you saying? You surely can't expect to stay here.' His glance fell on to the baby in her arms and he added somewhat musingly, 'Though I can see your predicament. Where have you come from? Can't you go back and return another day?'

'I've come from Salford. When I was changing trains in

Bolton, one of my bags was stolen – the bag with my money in it. I have only a few pounds put aside. I … I was hoping to come to some arrangement over Daisy today. I can see you have other concerns as well, and I am sorry about that, but I must settle what is to happen to Daisy.'

His eyebrows rose a fraction, in a gesture which implied acknowledgement of her situation and Bea unaccountably sensed a slight affinity with him. They were both facing a quandary: Mr Dearden was the one whom, she hoped, would resolve hers – but how was he going to resolve the other one? Her mind sprang ahead. She wasn't quite sure that she *knew* what she was saying, nor what she expected, but the words came out, anyway! 'Your difficulty obviously concerns your children, Mr Dearden. I'm sure they can't be as bad as Miss Winstanley said. Maybe I…?'

He stared at her. 'What are you suggesting, Miss Rossall?'

Bea took a deep breath, the audacity of what she was about to propose suddenly hit her – but what option had she? 'I … I have had some experience with children,' she began hesitantly. 'I ran a sort of day school in Salford. You seem suddenly to be in need of someone to take Miss Winstanley's place. I … I am offering to take her place … on a trial basis, of course.'

'You? But I know nothing about you – except that you have invaded my home and accused me of fathering your child.'

'Not *my* child, Mr Dearden. Elsie Brindle's child, Daisy. But, that aside, you seem to be in need of… a governess? Someone to take care of your children? I presume Mrs Dearden is not able to do so?'

Mr Dearden pressed his lips together. 'You presume quite rightly, Miss Rossall. To be precise, there is no Mrs Dearden. However, I am not sure I can accept your offer. How am I to

know what your character is? Have you any letters of recommendation?'

The fact that there was no Mrs Dearden made one aspect of
her mission here easier; that point hardly registered as his
reference to her stolen letter affirming her good character sank
in. Her shoulders sagged. 'I'm sorry. I did have one, but it was
in the bag that was stolen.'

'How convenient!'

His sarcasm hit Bea hard. 'No, it wasn't convenient at all,
sir!' she flashed in anger. 'I also lost most of my money and my
lunch! *And* it has put me in this predicament!'

Her response brought a flush to his cheeks. 'Yes,' he
conceded slowly. 'I am sorry. I spoke out of turn.' He stroked his
chin thoughtfully. 'I must admit, you sound educated.'

He was wavering, though still undecided, when Mrs Kellett
stormed back into the kitchen, her face like thunder. She
planted herself in front of Mr Dearden, her hands firmly on her
hips.

'Now, look 'ere, Mr Dearden! I'm not paid to look after those
children – and Nanny Adams was asleep in 'er room and 'adn't
'eard a thing! If you can't get someone to take better care of 'em
and teach 'em 'ow to behave, then I'm leavin'! I've worked 'ere
for nigh on thirty years but enough is enough! I'm not goin' to
put up wi' it any longer!'

For once in his life, Henry Dearden felt he was backed up
against a wall. Whatever he decided, it was going to affect his
life – a life that had been ordered and uncomplicated until his
brother had decided to flee to America, leaving *him*, a
confirmed bachelor and with no wish to change his status, in
charge of his two nieces. He glanced at Miss Rossall and
considered his options. It was either no governess nor
cook/housekeeper and two rebellious, troublesome girls on his

hands all day and all night – with no one but their elderly nursemaid to take care of them – or he could take a chance on this high-spirited young woman, whose attire placed her in the lower classes but whose speech revealed a competent education and whose presence would, perhaps, persuade Mrs Kellett to stay and would give him time to sort out a more lasting solution to his domestic predicament. In reality, he had no choice!

'You're quite right, Mrs Kellett,' he agreed, taking the wind out of her sails. 'Well, let us hope that our difficulties are over. I've just engaged Miss Rossall to be the children's governess – on a month's approval. Isn't that so, Miss Rossall?'

Bea's eyes widened, a flicker of hope springing within her. 'Y … yes, that's correct, Mr Dearden.'

'What? 'Er?' Mrs Kellett's disapproval was obvious. 'You don't know nothin' about 'er! And she's got a babby! For all you know, she may be—!'

'That's quite enough, Mrs Kellett!' Mr Dearden cut in. 'I will be looking into Miss Rossall's credentials but, for now, in the circumstances thrust upon us, we are taking each other on trust. Now, there are two letters I must write most urgently before Miss Winstanley leaves. Where have you left the children, Mrs Kellett?'

'In t'schoolroom,' Mrs Kellett said somewhat sullenly. She sniffed. 'Nanny Adams is with 'em now an' I warned 'em what'd 'appen if they move off them chairs.'

'Thank you, Mrs Kellett. Now, Miss Rossall, whilst I write my letters, perhaps you would like to take off your wet coat, and hang it over the back of a chair for now. Join me at the foot of the stairs in about twenty minutes' time and I will take you to meet my nieces.'

So saying, he slipped out of the kitchen, leaving Bea temporarily in Mrs Kellett's hands.

Hmm, so the children were his nieces, not his daughters. Did that make a difference? She didn't think so; he was obviously their guardian.

Mrs Kellett's eyes narrowed, as she swept her glance up and down Bea's form. Her lips curled into a sneer. 'Yer might 'ave 'oodwinked the master, miss, but yer won't find me such a push-over. I'll be keeping a close eye on you, I will – an' don't think I'm going to nursemaid tha babby!' She gave a harsh laugh. 'Yer'll soon be wishin' tha'd never come to Endmoor 'Ouse!'

Bea tried to smile at the woman, but found it difficult. 'I shall do my best to fulfil my obligations, Mrs Kellett. But, wouldn't it be better if we agree to respect each other's position?'

'Hmph!'

At that moment Gertie burst into the kitchen through the outer door, but pulled up abruptly when she saw Mrs Kellett. She quickly closed the door and stood uncertainly on the doormat.

Mrs Kellett turned her back on Bea, taking out her wrath on the kitchen-maid instead. 'There's no need to stand gawpin', Gertie!' she barked. 'Get yer coat off and set to work. There's a broken plate there to be swept up! It'll come out o' yer wages that will.'

'No, no, Mrs Kellett,' Bea felt impelled to interrupt. 'It wasn't Gertie's fault.'

Mrs Kellett swung back to face Bea again, her face red with anger. 'And whose fault was it then? Were you dryin' t'dishes, miss?'

'No, of course not,' Bea replied, 'but—'

'Then leave me to sort out me own kitchen. I say what 'appens in 'ere and yer'd best remember that – we've wasted enough time as it is. And when yer've finished t'dishes, Gertie, yer can start on t'pans! And mek sure I can see me face in 'em afore you're done!'

Gertie hurried forward, dropped to her knees and quickly began to brush up the broken crockery.

Bea knew she would only make matters worse if she argued further, so she unwrapped the shawl from around Daisy and laid the baby carefully on to the rocking-chair near the fire. Daisy's clothes were damp and needed to be changed. Bea quickly unfastened her valise and took out a flannelette nightgown, a towelling napkin, a knitted blanket and the last bottle of milk, which she placed on the table.

'Would you see that this is warmed to the right temperature whilst I change Daisy's clothes, Mrs Kellett?' she asked. There was no response. Bea pressed her lips together. If Mrs Kellett had shown any friendship towards her, she might have asked her to keep an eye on Daisy whilst she went upstairs to meet the children or asked the housekeeper what the children were like. Or even how many there were, for heaven's sake! Dear Lord, what had she let herself in for?

She swiftly changed Daisy into the dry clothes. Then cradling the baby in her arms, she went into the main part of the house and waited at the foot of the stairs as she had been bidden. The house had a distinctly masculine feel to it. The hall was dark and plain, though the upper walls were relieved by a selection of paintings: country scenes in sombre colours and a few portraits, no doubt of former Deardens, by the family resemblance. What the hallway needed was a splash of colour, Bea decided, or a vase of flowers, perhaps?

Her musing ended when Mr Dearden came out of a room part-way down the hall.

'Ah, Miss Rossall, perhaps you will tell Gertie to run upstairs and tell Miss Winstanley her cab is here?'

'Y … yes, of course.'

Bea involuntarily straightened her spine as she went back to the kitchen. She resisted the impulse to knock on the door – her position, albeit temporary and on-trial, was superior to that of a cook or housekeeper. She spoke pleasantly, but firmly as she repeated Mr Dearden's request.

Mrs Kellett responded with a disgruntled sniff. 'Hmph! Yer'd best get up there, then, Gertie – and no messin' about! There's work to be done!'

Bea stood aside as Gertie hurried past her. 'Thank you, Mrs Kellett.'

She returned to await Mr Dearden at the foot of the stairs. Gertie was the first to run down again. Shortly afterwards, a sound from above her made her aware that someone else was coming down the stairs. She glanced up. It was the departing governess, a large valise in one hand and a smaller one in the other.

After a brief hesitation, Miss Winstanley thrust out her chin and continued her descent. When she reached the bottom step she stopped and looked Beatrice up and down, her lips curling in scorn. 'If you are thinking of taking my place, let me warn you that his nieces are a pair of wild heathens who are completely out of control! No governess with self-respect would even consider taking them on!'

Bea was taken aback by the governess's vehemence. 'I will do my best,' she said quietly.

'Hmph!' The woman's lips curled with derision as she let her eyes glance over Bea, resting on the baby in her arms. 'Well, I can only imagine what sort of person *you* might be! On your own head be it.' And with that remark still hanging in the air, she swung past Bea and strode along the hallway to a seat near the front door.

A feeling of unease swept through Bea. Was she going to regret her impetuous action? Bea watched as Mr Dearden spoke to the departing governess and handed her two envelopes. The woman snapped, 'I should hope so!'

Mr Dearden opened the inner front door and ushered Miss Winstanley ahead of him. After she had departed, he closed the door with an air of finality and stood immobile for a moment. Bea supposed he was taking a deep breath and composing his thoughts. She was struggling to compose her own. Had she done the right thing? It was too late to back out now – Mr Dearden had turned and was striding towards her.

'Ah, Miss Rossall!' He spoke with forced cheerfulness as he strode along the hallway. 'Ready to meet my nieces, I see. Good! Come with me.' He started to ascend the stairway.

Bea followed him, her mind full of questions. 'Are they here without their parents?'

He halted his steps as he replied and turned to face her. 'Sadly, my brother, Frederick is a widower. His wife died six months ago whilst Freddie was travelling in America. He hasn't yet returned home.'

'Oh! Maybe the news hasn't reached him yet? I'm sure he will come, once he knows. Any father would....' Her voice trailed away. Of what use were such platitudes? She knew nothing of the man.

'All I can say is that he has been informed. But, that is *my* concern, not yours.'

His tone deterred further comment on the matter and Bea hastened to apologize 'Of course. I'm sorry.' She must learn to remember her place here. She was a mere employee, and, as such, had no right to question her employer on personal matters. However, questions about the children were a different matter. 'How old are the children?' she asked as she began to follow him up the stairs.

'Winifred is ten and Lily is eight. They ...' He paused, obviously trying to choose his words carefully. 'They haven't yet adjusted to their loss. Their behaviour is ... well, a little wild, I'm afraid, and their nursemaid is too old to wield much authority. I am a bachelor and I don't find it easy to communicate with young children. I shall expect you to keep the girls occupied and out of my way.'

'That sounds a little heartless, Mr Dearden,' Bea couldn't stop herself from saying. 'Surely, they just need someone to show them a little affection and give them some stability in their lives.' Oh, dear, there she went again. She was going to find being servile very difficult.

Mr Dearden glanced down at her, an eyebrow raised. 'And you think you can do that, Miss Rossall? Quite a few have tried and given up in failure. Take Miss Winstanley, for example.'

'Hmm.' Bea considered the sour-faced woman who had just left the household. 'Children need to know they are loved if they are to thrive, especially when their mother has been taken away when they arc so young – and their father is unable to be with them.'

'I detect a note of criticism, Miss Rossall. Well, you have the opportunity to prove your theory. I must admit that, so far, I have found the governesses I have employed either too weak or too harsh. You propose a middle road, do you? I hope you succeed. All I want is a quiet household. I am a professional draughtsman and am extremely busy in my work at present. I cannot afford to be interrupted all day long by a list of complaints about my nieces' behaviour. I *know* they are badly behaved – and unco-operative and sullen. I don't need to be reminded of those facts twenty times each day! On my brother's return, whenever that may be, I would like to hand them over to him in a much improved condition. You are silent, Miss Rossall. Are you already regretting your impulsive offer to tutor them?"

Chapter 5

'N... NO,' BEA denied, though, in truth, she *was* questioning her wisdom in thinking to resolve her situation in this way. How on earth had Elsie ever become enamoured of this heartless man? They made a most unlikely couple. Or had she been forcibly 'taken' and had later imagined herself to have been wooed? He was handsome enough to have turned the maid's head if he had sought to do so ... but, somehow, that putative role didn't seem to sit as firmly as she had expected. Surely Elsie hadn't mistaken the name? She had sounded so sure and had saved the newspaper cutting as some sort of memento.

Bea shook herself free of her musings, realizing that Mr Dearden was again striding up the wide stairway with little regard for her own shorter stride. She increased her pace and caught up with him as the stairway turned towards the front of the house. Mr Dearden strode off along the left-hand corridor, giving brief descriptions of what lay behind each door they passed, indicating left and right. 'Mrs Kellett's room ... the nursery suite ... the bathroom for this wing; you will find the linen cupboard in there as well. The room you will be using is the one on the right at the end. I doubt Mrs Kellett will have time to sort it out before dinner. Obviously, with Miss Winstanley leaving so abruptly ...' He didn't bother to complete the sentence.

'That will present no difficulty. I will change the sheets myself,' Bea assured him, only too thankful to have a dry bed to sleep in that night. It was more than she had hoped for.

'And here is the schoolroom.'

He stood back to allow Bea to enter in front of him. She stepped into a fair-sized room of uninspiring appearance. Its mid-green walls were the backdrop to a number of dark-brown cupboards and a few small tables bearing untidy piles of paper and boxes of pencils. Another table held a vase containing a few stalks of brown leaves, with a pile of stones and pieces of tree bark in a heap at one side. At the side of the room was a table covered with oilcloth on which overturned paintpots had spilled out their contents, some of which was dripping on to the floor – the source of the vivid splashes of colour that disfigured the room.

A large steel-meshed fireguard guarded a meagre fire that barely took the chill off the room. The item of furniture nearest to the fire was a wooden rocking-chair, surrounded by screwed-up balls of paper – the 'missiles', no doubt – and two skipping-ropes tied together and left tangled on the floor. A teacher's desk stood next beside a free-standing blackboard and a smaller, double-seated desk stood in the centre of the room facing the blackboard.

Two girls were seated at the double desk. They were dressed in identical long-sleeved brown woollen frocks covered by brown-and-white-checked aprons. Their hands, their hair, their sullen faces and clothes were smeared with paint. Standing by was the elderly nursemaid, her expression shamefaced – but with a glint in her eyes that Bea suspected was born of an urge to protect her misbehaved charges.

As the two adults entered the room, the younger girl, her fair hair pulled back into tight plaits, slid along her wooden seat to be closer to her elder sister. The older girl's hair was a mass of chestnut curls that had long since sprung out of the clips that had held them in place.

The nursemaid eyed Bea with some curiosity, but it was Mr Dearden to whom she spoke. 'Eh, Mr Dearden, my little lambs didn't mean no harm.' Her voice quavered.

Mr Dearden stood a couple of feet away and swung his gaze around the disorderly scene, his expression severe. 'Didn't they? That isn't what Miss Winstanley supposed.'

He busied himself by lighting a few extra gas-jets positioned around the room, though the added light thus given failed to enhance the depressing dullness of the room. In the increased illumination, Bea saw the expression on the older girl's face harden as she waited for him to speak again. That would be Winifred, she remembered. She suspected the girls were expecting a severe punishment, a suspicion borne out when Winifred folded her arms across her chest with an air of defiance and glowered darkly.

'Well, I can see why Miss Winstanley was so upset!' Mr Dearden eventually remarked, his voice showing exasperation more than anger, Bea considered. 'This schoolroom is a disgrace – and your behaviour more so. It is quite inexcusable to treat your governess in such a manner. What have you to say about it, Winifred?'

Winifred pressed her lips together and stared ahead.

'I demand an answer, Winifred. I cannot allow such behaviour from you. Your punishment will be all the more severe if you refuse to give an answer.'

Winifred glanced sideways at her sister. Lily twisted her lips wryly, her cheeks burning brightly. Winifred dropped her gaze. 'It was only a game,' she muttered. 'We weren't actually going to *do* anything.'

Mr Dearden raised an eyebrow. 'Such as scalping Miss Winstanley? I sincerely hope not! The spoken threat was serious enough. In fact, she feels so badly treated that she has resigned from her post.'

A gleam of satisfaction in Winifred's eyes caused him to raise a challenging eyebrow and hold her gaze, his expression unwavering. 'If that was your intention, you will be surprised to learn that Miss Rossall has agreed to take the position of your governess.'

Winifred's head whipped round to stare at Bea. Her surprise turned into a glare of hatred. Lily's glance was more subdued, curious rather than hostile.

Mr Dearden smiled grimly. 'Yes, Winifred. That was opportune, was it not?' He turned to face Bea. 'Miss Rossall, here are my nieces, Winifred and Lily. I'm sorry to have to leave you to sort out this disorder but I have a drawing I need to complete this afternoon and I have wasted enough time already. Winifred, Lily, under Miss Rossall's supervision you will clean up the schoolroom. Any further bad behaviour will result in your punishment being doubled. Understood? Good! I will leave you to it, Miss Rossall. If you will hand over the child to Nanny Adams, I am sure she will take care of her whilst you set my nieces to sort out this disgraceful mess.'

'Yessir,' Nanny Adams murmured, throwing a doubtful look at Bea.

Bea glanced down at the still-sleeping Daisy. It tore at her heart to have to place her in Nanny's arms but she did as she was bidden. 'She should sleep for a couple of hours,' she murmured. 'If she gets upset ...' A tremor in her voice made her take a firm hold on herself and she said in a firmer voice, 'She is a very placid baby. I am sure you will have no trouble with her.'

'Ee, that's all right, miss.'

'Good. Then we will leave you to it, Miss Rossall.' Mr Dearden opened the schoolroom door. 'Come, Nanny Adams. Miss Rossall will introduce herself more fully to you later.'

With a lingering glance at the two girls, Nanny Adams hobbled out of the room, with Mr Dearden following behind, leaving Bea to cope with the situation as best as she could. It wasn't the ideal way to start to gain the trust of these motherless girls. She felt Mr Dearden's attitude had been a blend of controlled anger and cool detachment. If *that* was the way he conducted himself, it was no wonder there was no Mrs Dearden! Her doubts were growing about him being an ideal father for Daisy. Had he no warmth of affection for his nieces?

However, there were more pressing matters to deal with – in the form of two bewildered and rebellious little girls. She smiled at them and turned round slowly, taking in the paint-splashed walls and floor. 'Well, you obviously wanted to brighten up your classroom – but I'm not sure I *quite* like your method of doing so.' She paused and again surveyed the room, the first finger of her right hand against her cheek. 'It *is* a bit dark in here. Once we have cleared up this mess, we must think of a way to make the room a bit brighter, don't you agree, Winifred?'

She held her gaze on Winifred's face, making it clear that she expected an answer.

'I s'pose so,' Winifred eventually muttered, with a shrug of her shoulders. Her facial expression remained rebellious.

'What about you, Lily?' Bea eyed the drab, brown curtains. 'New curtains, perhaps? What colour would you like them to be? Yellow?'

'Was that a real baby?' Lily asked, ignoring her question.

'Yes, of course. Do you like babies?'

'I don't know. I had a doll – but Miss Winstanley made me put it in a box and she put it on top of her wardrobe. She said we are too big now to have dolls, didn't she, Winnie?'

'I don't want a doll. Dolls are for babies.' Winifred replied. 'And I don't like babies, either.'

'Oh, I'm sure you'll like Daisy. She's a good little baby. You can help me bath her later, if you like. And I'll show you how to give her her bottle of milk.'

'Is she *your* baby?' Lily asked.

'No. Sadly, her mama died soon after she was born – so I look after her,' Bea explained gently.

'Our mama died, too,' Lily confided, ignoring Winifred's scowls. 'And Papa's gone away to 'Merica. That's why we came here.'

'I'm sure he'll be back soon,' Bea tried to reassure her. 'In the meantime, we have to get on with the situation we find ourselves in – and the first thing we have to do, as Mr Dearden has told us, is to tidy up this room.'

'He's called Uncle Henry,' Lily informed her. 'I don't think he likes us very much.'

Bea's heart contracted at that simple statement but she felt compelled to defend their uncle. 'He isn't used to children – but I'm sure he will like you when he gets to know you better, especially if you show him how nice you can be.'

'Huh! I don't want him to like us,' Winifred commented. 'We are only here until Papa comes back to take us home.'

'And won't he be surprised when he sees how much you have grown while he has been away!' Bea tried to cheer them. 'Now, let's get to work. The sooner we start, the sooner we finish.'

Winifred was cajoled into showing Bea where to find a bucket, three scrubbing brushes and some cloths and they set to work – Lily with an eagerness to please, Winifred more reluctantly. As things were tidied away, Bea was concerned to see very little in the way of books and other educational equipment. Presumably the governesses had used their own teaching aids and had taken them with them. She would need to make good use of her imagination to provide an interesting teaching programme for Winifred and Lily.

Eventually, a glance at the schoolroom clock showed it to be almost five o'clock. 'Where do you have your tea?' she asked, knowing Daisy would soon be yelling lustily for her next bottle.

'In here, at that table,' Winifred said, scowling again as she pointed to the table they had wiped clean of paint. 'And it's usually cold by the time we get it.'

'Right!' said Bea, not impressed with that arrangement. 'Well, it's quite chilly in here. I think we will go down to the kitchen and ask if we can have it there. And afterwards we can take Daisy's bottle to Nanny Adams. Let's go and wash our hands in the bathroom – and present ourselves to Mrs Kellett. You deserve a treat after all your hard work.'

'Do we?' Lily asked eagerly. 'Do you think we might get some jam on our bread. We sometimes used to before Miss Winstanley came.'

'I don't see why not,' Bea surmised. 'And I happen to know that Mrs Kellet made some lovely scones this afternoon.'

Winifred's eyes brightened for a moment, until she quickly suppressed the gleam. Nevertheless, Bea felt some hope that all the girls needed was some love and praise and she could give plenty of that.

Mrs Kellett thought differently. Her eyes hardened as Bea made her request. 'No, yer can't! Yer'll be in me way,' she snapped. 'I'm busy preparing the master's dinner. Besides, children's teas should be taken in the schoolroom. It were good enough for Miss Winstanley and all t'others. An' yer'll 'ave to tek your teas upstairs yerself. I can't be sparin' Gertie after all th'upset this afternoon!'

Bea glanced at the kitchen table, where a prepared tray stood ready. It had on it a few slices of buttered bread, four eggs in egg-cups, four dishes of jelly, a teapot, two cups and saucers and two glasses of milk. 'Very well. We will join Nanny Adams in the day nursery.' Bea strove to keep her voice light. 'Oh, and we would all like some of your delicious scones, Mrs Kellett. The girls have worked hard cleaning up the schoolroom.'

Mrs Kellett slammed four scones on to a plate and pushed it towards Bea, her expression foreboding. 'An' I s'pose yer'll be wantin' jam an' all?' she said sarcastically.

Bea smiled. 'That would be very nice, Mrs Kellett. Thank you. Oh, and I see Daisy's bottle is ready, too. Will you carry the bottle, Winifred? Good. Come with me.'

Leaving the frosty atmosphere behind them, they returned upstairs, where Bea introduced herself to Nanny Adams and told her they would be having their meals in the nursery from now on. 'It is far pleasanter to eat in here than in the school-room,' she said, glancing round. The nursery was a light, airy room that overlooked the front of the house and had doors on opposite sides. Bea correctly took these doors to be the girls' bedroom on one side and Nanny Adams's bedroom on the other. A merry fire burned in the grate, protected by a sturdy fire-guard. Drawn to face the fire were two easy chairs and a small sofa. Daisy, cosily wrapped up in a shawl, was sleeping on one of the chairs, wedged between two cushions.

Nanny Adams indicated the table near the window. 'It's where we 'ave our breakfast,' she commented as she made room for the tray. At first cool in her welcome, she warmed to Bea when Bea explained that Daisy was the daughter of a lately-deceased servant-girl, and was now in her care. 'Eeh, well, it's grand to have a babby in t'nursery once more – an' she's be'n no trouble. Where'll she sleep, though? I'm not sure there's a cradle 'ere for 'er. I doubt there's be'n a babby 'ere since Mr Frederick.'

'I'm sure we'll find something.' Bea smiled. 'I thought the girls might enjoy playing with Daisy for a short while after they've eaten their tea. We'll finish tidying the schoolroom tomorrow. What d'you say, girls? And then you can help to get her ready for bed.'

Lily, leaning over the chair where Daisy lay, eagerly nodded her head. 'Ooh, yes. That'll be lovely, won't it, Winnie?'

Winifred tossed her head and turned away. 'I'm hungry. Are we having our tea, now?'

Bea wondered why Winifred was so antagonistic towards Daisy. Was she jealous of the attention she was getting? She hoped it would pass when she felt more familiar with Daisy. 'Yes. Come and sit down. Will you say grace, Nanny Adams?'

During the meal Bea was able to draw out some conversation from both girls, aided by Nanny Adams's gentle prompting. She learned that the children's mother's parents were still alive but Mrs Sharratt, the grandmother, had suffered a stroke. From Nanny's guarded expression as she imparted the information, Bea gathered there was more to be said about the circumstances but she didn't press for details with the girls present.

'Mr Sharratt owns a shoe factory near Blackburn but now spends most of his time looking after his wife,' Nanny explained, adding, 'though he's been to visit once.'

'Well, maybe he will come again once the weather gets warmer,' Bea suggested, thinking it would be good for the girls to see other members of their family.

Whimpers from Daisy brought the meal to an end and Bea

went to gather the infant into her arms. She took her over to the table. 'See, she's wide awake now and she's looking at you both. She's wondering who you are. Come and sit on the sofa and watch how I give Daisy her bottle.'

'You said we could feed her, too,' Lily reminded her.

'All right. Winifred, why don't you try first?' Bea suggested. 'Sit on one of the easy chairs and I'll pass Daisy to you.'

Winifred scowled and stood with her arms rigidly at her side. 'I don't want to,' she refused, her face set. 'I told you, I don't like babies.'

'Eh, now, don't be like that, Miss Winnie,' Nanny Adams cajoled. 'I don't know what's got into her, Miss Rossall.'

'Never mind. Another time, maybe?' Bea turned to Lily. 'Come on then, Lily.'

Lily quickly seated herself. Bea propped a cushion under her elbow and gently placed Daisy in her arms. 'Look! She's smiling at me!' Lily exclaimed. 'See, Winnie! Isn't she lovely? I think she likes me. Look, Winnie!'

Winifred shrugged but didn't make any move to go closer to Daisy. 'She's just a baby. Babies smile at anyone. She doesn't *know* you.'

'She soon will, Miss Winnie,' Nanny Adams assured her. 'I can remember how you loved to see Lily's face light up when you came into t'nursery to play with her. Eh, it takes me back. Of course, Lily's hair was fair but I think Daisy's going to be dark, like you.'

'Lily's my sister. That's why I liked playing with her,' Winifred said loftily. 'Daisy's just a baby. *Anyone*'s baby. She's nothing to do with me.'

Bea felt her heart contract. Only *she* suspected how closely Daisy was related to Winifred and Lily – but she mustn't speak of it until the matter had been settled with Mr Dearden. Did

Nanny Adams see a family resemblance? *Had* Winifred looked like Daisy? Would that help Mr Dearden to accept her? Or would it make him send her away so that no one else would suspect the reality? She would find out, later.

Winifred moved away and squatted down beside a large doll's house that stood against the wall. She began to rearrange the furniture in the rooms. Bea wondered again whether Winifred felt excluded by the attention Daisy was getting. She followed Winifred across the room. 'That's a very nice house, Winifred. Did you bring it from your home?'

'Yes.' Her voice was flat and Bea was surprised when she added more. 'We had lots of toys there but we couldn't bring them all. Uncle Henry only let us bring those we wanted most and this was my favourite.'

'I can tell. You have looked after it nicely and collected a lot of furniture. Have you given names to the people in your house?'

Slowly, reluctantly almost, Winifred named the figures. There were only three. Two children called Molly and Dolly, and a female adult who, Winifred said, was Nanny Adams. No amount of cajoling could persuade Winifred to say any more and Bea reluctantly left her to play alone while she wandered round the nursery dayroom. She was glad to see it was better stocked than the schoolroom.

She continued slowly round the room. She was pleased to see that the toy cupboard had open shelves with a selection of toys. There were some boxes of building-bricks; some board games – Ludo and Snakes and Ladders; a Jack-in-the-box; some puppets; some stacking toys; and a few balls and other catching games. And, on a high shelf, a wooden box with its lid closed. Bea picked it up, curious to see what was inside. Oh! It contained some more small figures that belonged to the doll's house. Winifred must have forgotten about these. She turned eagerly, moving back towards the girl. 'Look, Winifred! There are some more figures here. See, there's a man and a lady and even a little baby and a cradle.'

Winifred's face closed. 'I don't need any more,' she replied quite coldly. She angled her body away from Bea and made no further response.

Bea grimaced wryly, making an apologetic shrug towards Nanny Adams. Of course. The figures were the mama and papa, both of whom were now missing from the children's lives. And a non-existent baby whose presence would invade the smaller family unit that was now their lot. That unit obviously didn't include their Uncle Henry.

Her heart felt heavy as she glanced towards Winifred. Her mother's death and her father's absence had made a great impression on her life and she suspected that Winifred was attempting to withdraw from its harsh reality. Would she be able to help her to come to terms with her loss? She hoped so, but it would take a great deal of sensitive handling – providing, of course, she were allowed to stay after her coming interview with Mr Dearden.

Chapter 6

LATER, AFTER DAISY had been bathed, Bea left her in the care of Nanny Adams and the girls while she went to her room. Her valise had been carried up, though, by whom, Bea didn't know. A pair of sheets had also been placed upon her bed and the mantles lit.

Bea glanced around. It was a pleasant room, divided by a heavy curtain that was partly drawn across the room, revealing a single bed beyond the curtain.

The sitting area had a plain, square rug on the floor, a wooden chair positioned at a small round table, a small cupboard by the side-window and, nearer to the small fireplace, an easy chair. Neither the table nor the cupboard were large enough to allow her to prepare the girls' schoolwork on them. She must be expected to do that in the schoolroom, she supposed.

In the further portion of the room a chest of drawers, adorned by a free-standing mirror, stood underneath the window. Bea walked over to the window and peered out into the cold, wet night, discovering that her room overlooked the front of the house. She drew the curtains across the window and turned to survey the room with some satisfaction. The bed was tucked against the inner wall, with a cut-cloth rug on the floor beside it. Against the outer wall of the house stood a small wardrobe with a box on top. Ah, yes, the girls' dolls. She would give them back to the girls before their bedtime.

First, though, a cot of some sort for Daisy. Ah, yes! The lower section of the wardrobe was a drawer. She pulled it out and laid it on the floor and then lined it with one of the blankets from her bed, leaving enough of the blanket to fold back over the top as a cover. There, that would do nicely!

Daisy slept through being transferred to her makeshift cot and Bea sank on to the bed. Was it really only twelve hours since she had left Salford? So much had happened. And it wasn't over yet. She still had to face the interview with Mr Dearden.

She changed into her only other suitable day frock and tidied her hair. As she replaced her spectacles, she grimaced at the prim, severe reflection in the mirror. It seemed to belong to someone else – but it was the image she had chosen to hide behind. She would have to get used to it.

Looking far calmer than she felt, she descended the stairs and knocked on the door of the room from which she had earlier seen Mr Dearden emerge. However, it was a door opposite that opened and Bea turned to see Mr Dearden framed in the doorway. He was wearing a loose-fitting dark-brown jacket over a matching waistcoat, and lighter brown trousers. Showing above his waistcoat was a carefully knotted dark-brown tie. Bea was glad she had changed.

'Will you join me in my sitting room, Miss Rossall?' Mr Dearden invited, holding open the door as she passed through. He gestured towards a firmly cushioned armchair at the left of the fireplace, where a well-banked fire glowed brightly. 'Please, be seated.'

Bea seated herself on the edge of the chair, her back straight and her hands clasped in her lap. Once more she was reminded of the events that had taken place in Mr Ackroyd's house and she couldn't help a tremor of nerves shuddering through her body. However, Mr Dearden didn't tower over her. He seated himself opposite her and leaned back in his chair, his hands lightly clasped across his waistcoat, his eyes calmly regarding her.

Beatrice found the silence a little unnerving. Unconsciously, she tilted her chin a little higher, and after a moment's pause she raised her eyes to his and silently returned his appraisal through her out-of-focus lenses. His expression seemed open and genuinely interested. His eyes were dark brown; his hair, also dark, was cut short at the back and sides but a lock at the front fell in a disarming way over his forehead. Apart from a small moustache, he was clean-shaven. It struck her again that he wasn't at all the sort of man she had expected to find.

Mr Dearden leaned forward and said, 'Tell me something about yourself, Miss Rossall. Since you have no letters of reference, give me the chance to allow my instinct to judge your character.'

Bea swallowed. 'I ... I am twenty-five years of age,' she began hesitantly. 'My father was the vicar of St Peter's Church of England parish in Salford until his death four weeks ago. My mother died when I was almost twelve years old. I have no living brothers or sisters. The ones born after me died in infancy. My father, being a natural scholar and teacher, educated me as he would have educated a son. Thus I have knowledge, though rudimentary by academic standards, of many subjects including philosophy, mathematics, the classics and history; and a fuller knowledge of the scriptures in various translations. Even though no one has so far seen fit to employ me on the strength of my education, I feel I am qualified to teach these subjects to children, to prepare them for the rigours of a more professional education. I did, indeed, begin a day school for some of the poor children in Papa's parish.'

'Really?' Mr Dearden cocked his head on one side. 'So, in spite of finding that your education has not fitted you for the sort of employment you would have wished, you consider putting yourself in the position of perpetuating the folly of educating females?'

Bea bristled. Was he yet another man who considered females to be inferior to men? Feeling discomposed by the effrontery of his criticism, Bea snatched off her spectacles, bringing his features into focus. 'Yes!' she said sharply. 'I do so in the hope that, one day, women will have the same opportunities as men – brain versus brain; not brain versus brawn!'

A flicker of interest crossed Mr Dearden's face and a glimmer of admiration in his eyes momentarily startled Bea. She belatedly realized that she held her spectacles in her hand. Flustered, she fumbled for her handkerchief and made a show of polishing the lenses, before returning her spectacles to sit uncomfortably on her nose. She glared at the man. She didn't want him to find her attractive. Attraction led to indiscretion and she didn't want any more of that, thank you very much!

Mr Dearden laughed, causing the wrinkles at the edges of his eyes to deepen – which quite transformed his face, softening the severity. If she hadn't been feeling quite so agitated, Bea might have found his softened features engaging. As it was, she stiffened her spine and increased her glare. Was he laughing at *her* or at the words she had spoken?

'I suspect you were born a few generations too soon, Miss Rossall,' Mr Dearden commented drily, then continued, 'Have you no subjects of greater value to offer to females of *this* generation?'

Bea relaxed slightly, realizing it had been her words that had caused his amusement. That was easier to cope with. 'I enjoy painting, sewing and music and I have also had the practical experience of running a home for my father – with the help of Mrs Hurst, our housekeeper,' she admitted stiffly.

Mr Dearden inclined his head slightly, impressed by her response. 'Did you try to gain employment nearer to your home?'

Bea gazed at him frankly. 'I did – but no one wanted to employ me with a baby to care for. I had promised Elsie, you see. I couldn't abandon her – though a number of prospective employers callously suggested that I put her in the workhouse.'

'Ah yes! We come to the question of the child.'

'Daisy,' Bea insisted. 'Her name is Daisy.'

'So it is. And what makes you think I am Daisy's father?'

'Elsie named you. "Mr Dearden of Endmoor House in Horwich." She had a newspaper cutting which included your full name – Mr Henry Dearden. I brought it with me – but it was stolen, along with my purse and other things on my journey here today.'

'A newspaper cutting with my name in it doesn't make me responsible for fathering a child, Miss Rossall,' Mr Dearden said calmly. 'Your maidservant was mistaken in naming me as the man who ruined her. What did you say her name was?'

Bea wasn't surprised by his denial. She had expected it – but she didn't intend to back down at the first hurdle. 'She was called Elsie Brindle and was the daughter of a poor but respectable family who allowed her to go into service with a family at Breightmet whose surname is Martland.'

A tiny flicker of recognition seemed to flicker in Mr

Dearden's eyes, strengthening Bea's resolve – but his next words didn't acknowledge his guilt. Instead, he said coolly, 'I have never met anyone with the name of Elsie Brindle. Neither have I ever stayed at the Martlands' home.'

Bea's heart sank at Mr Dearden's words. She could hardly call him a liar. She had no proof, other than Elsie's assertion. Was he lying? Or had Elsie somehow been mistaken?

Before she could compose her thoughts, Mr Dearden continued, 'I presume that is where the indiscretion is supposed to have taken place?'

Bea's anger at Elsie's betrayal reignited. 'It was not a "supposed" indiscretion, Mr Dearden! It was a very real violation of a young maidservant, innocent of the ways of men! Do not seek to make it less serious than it was. It cost that young girl her reputation and her life!'

'Really? And how am I to know that this child isn't yours and that of some ruffian who refuses to acknowledge his responsibilities?'

Bea's face flamed with anger and embarrassment. 'I am not in the habit of lying, sir!'

'Aren't you? But, as I know nothing about you, apart from what you have seen fit to tell me, how am I to be certain of that without references?'

Bea felt her cheeks flush again – but her common sense compelled her to acknowledge the truth of his words, inwardly at least. She held her head high and forced herself to look straight into his eyes, however unfocused they seemed to her. 'References cannot always be relied upon, Mr Dearden. I suspect many a glowing reference hides a desire to hand a troublesome employee elsewhere.'

A glimmer of amusement glowed momentarily in the depths of Mr Dearden's eyes but he merely inclined his head slightly by way of unspoken agreement. 'Have you such a jaded view of mankind, Miss Rossall? What about "judge not, that ye be not judged"?'

Bea bowed her head in assent. 'Yes, you are right.' She sighed but then tilted her chin high again, adding, 'But, since I must take your word that you are not Daisy's father, I expect the same courtesy to be granted towards me.'

Her voice was steady but, with the words spoken, the fight suddenly drained out of her as she realized that the consquence of accepting that Mr Dearden wasn't Daisy's father meant she had made a wasted journey and was left with no possible chance of ever discovering the name of Daisy's father. She had intended to refuse to accept any such denial but her instinct led her to believe this man. Wearily, she accepted defeat.

'I'm sorry to have wasted your time, Mr Dearden. I accept that Elsie must have been mistaken in naming you. I suppose *any* young man could have *pretended* to be you. I am sorry to have defamed your character. Thank you, at least, for listening to me and giving me and Daisy shelter for the night.' She rose from the chair. 'We will leave first thing in the morning. Goodnight.'

Mr Dearden stood also. 'Not so fast, Miss Rossall! You are forgetting our agreement!'

'Pardon?'

'You have agreed to a month's trial in the position of governess to my two nieces. Are you now reneging on that agreement?'

Bea was thrown into confusion. 'I assumed you would rather be rid of any reminder of my accusation.'

'Since we have both been guilty of wrong assumptions and have agreed to accept the veracity of each other's denial, I suggest we let bygones be bygones and start afresh. I am standing by my offer to you, subject to the same month's trial and confirmation of your good character when I have communication with whoever it was who wrote the reference that was stolen. You will be paid the same salary as I paid your predecessors, monthly, in arrears.'

Bea realized that she was shaking. She rested a hand on the back of the chair to steady herself. 'Oh! Then, y … yes, I accept. Thank you, Mr Dearden. I … I shall do my best not to let you down.'

'I hope so. As to Daisy's parentage—'

'I'm sorry. I should have approached the problem with more tact,' Bea interrupted. She felt her face flame with embarrassment again. How *could* she have accused him of being Daisy's father without being absolutely sure of her facts? He would have been quite within his rights if he had decided to throw her and Daisy out on to the street. She was thankful that he had chosen not to do so. 'I … I shall rear Daisy as my own. I don't mind. Really I don't. She is a lovely child.'

She paused, suddenly aware that she had interrupted him. How often had her father told her to listen to the full statement before giving an opinion? 'I'm sorry. You were saying?'

He shook his head. 'Nothing of any present consequence,' he conceded mildly. 'Now, if you will excuse me, I have some letters to write.'

'Of course,' Bea agreed. She needed to clean her travelling dress, be ready to give Daisy her next feed and then get herself to bed.

'Oh, before you go, since tomorrow is Saturday, may I suggest you take some time to get to know my nieces,' Mr Dearden surprised her by saying, adding, 'After they have both written a letter of apology to Miss Winstanley, of course. Their apologies must be in their best handwriting, with correct spelling and punctuation.'

'Y ... yes. Thank you. I will do that. Goodnight, Mr Dearden.'

Bea took her leave, leaving Mr Dearden alone in his sitting room.

He didn't stay there long. He crossed the hall into his study, the room he used as his workplace for the technical drawings he produced for the local locomotive works and for any other business he needed to conduct. He had two letters to write. The first, to Mrs Martland at Breightmet Hall, he worded carefully, enquiring whether a maidservant called Elsie Brindle had been in service there the previous year. The second, to his brother Freddie, care of a forwarding address in America, he wrote more swiftly, berating his brother once more for his past conduct and present lack of paternal care – and demanding a definite date for his proposed return to England.

Chapter 7

THE NEXT DAY started badly when Bea presented herself in the kitchen for her breakfast tray and Daisy's early-morning bottle. Mrs Kellett didn't hold back her evident disapproval of Bea's newly acquired position in the household.

'Don't think I don't know what yer're up to, miss!' she pronounced sourly. 'You might 'ave fooled t'master into takin' you on, with yer nasty insinuations – but you've chosen the wrong one there and no mistake! An' he already 'as a nice young lady, so don't you be causing no trouble! I'll be keepin' me eye on you, I will, so don't you forget it.'

Bea felt her face flush. However, she knew she had brought the condemnation upon herself by blurting out her accusation against Mr Dearden in front of Gertie – and she couldn't blame the girl for having repeated what she had heard. It was only right and proper that the servants' first loyalties were to their master.

'Mr Dearden and I have sorted out the misunderstanding,' she quietly assured Mrs Kellett, 'and I appreciate the opportunity he has given me. You needn't fear that I have any ulterior motive in taking up the position of governess. I intend to repay his generosity of spirit by serving him well.'

'Hmm! Like I said, we'll see about that! I'll be watchin'!'

Bea had no doubt that she would. She was thankful that her

tray was ready to be taken upstairs and escaped with it to her room.

Later, after feeding Daisy and eating her breakfast she went to the nursery to collect Winifred and Lily. The rain looked set to continue throughout the day and Bea made use of their enforced stay indoors by finishing tidying up the schoolroom whilst Winifred and Lily completed their letters of apology to their former governess.

At eleven o'clock Bea took the girls to the nursery day room to reassure herself that looking after Daisy was not too much for Nanny Adams to cope with. She discovered that Nanny Adams had already procured a bottle of warmed milk from the kitchen and was contentedly feeding the infant. Nanny was surprised to see the children, as they didn't normally get a mid-morning drink.

'What nonsense!' Bea declared. 'Everyone needs a hot drink in this weather. I will go and get them myself.' Oh dear, another confrontation was due, she supposed. She was right.

'What do you want now?' Mrs Kellett greeted her. 'I can't be doing with interruptions for anything to do with th'schoolroom. Miss Winstanley never came down here in t'middle o' t'morning.'

'Maybe she didn't, Mrs Kellett but I am here now and since no one told me of the arrangements you have for mid-morning and mid-afternoon drinks for the children, may I suggest that you send up enough milk to the nursery at the start of the day so that Nanny Adams can make drinks for us all when she makes her own? And a plate of biscuits, too, please.'

With a loud sniff, Mrs Kellett banged a jug of milk on to the table. 'That'll 'ave to do. The biscuits are over there.'

With a murmured, 'Thank you,' Bea took some biscuits out of the tin, put them on to a plate and carefully carried them and the jug of milk upstairs. Lily was crying when she re-entered the nursery and Nanny Adams was jogging Daisy up and down against her shoulder. Daisy's little mouth was trembling and Nanny Adams looked flustered. 'It was just a bit of disagreement, Miss Rossall,' she explained. 'It's all this wet weather putting them out of sorts.'

Bea glanced at the girls. Lily was glaring at her sister in an accusing way and Winifred was feigning indifference.

'Then let's hope the weather improves tomorrow. Maybe this drink and a biscuit will improve your tempers. I'll play with Daisy while you have your cup of tea, Nanny Adams, and then I'll take the girls back to the schoolroom. I want to see how well they can write and draw.'

She placed Daisy on a blanket on the rug by the nursery fire, where she was soon gurgling with pleasure again and waving her arms and legs in the air. She even tried to roll on to her side when Bea moved aside to pick up the cup of tea that Nanny Adams had poured for her, earning herself some exclamations of praise.

'Well, isn't she a quick one!' Nanny Adams declared. 'She'll be rolling right over before too long. She's you all over again, Miss Winnie. You were up and round the nursery before we had time to blink!'

'Wasn't I a quick one?' Lily asked, not wanting to be left out.

Nanny Adams chuckled. 'You were never given much chance, Miss Lily. You'd only to wave your arms in the direction of any toy and Miss Winnie would fetch it to you. She'd have carried you about, if I'd let her.' She patted the elder girl's arm affectionately. 'You were such a good girl. A big help to me and your dear mama.'

The start of a faint blush of pleasure had begun to colour Winifred's cheeks at Nanny Adams's praise but it faded away abruptly at the mention of her mama and her features closed again.

Bea knew the girl was hurting deep inside. She longed to sweep her up into her arms and comfort her but she knew she would have to earn that right before Winifred would be ready to respond to such a personal gesture. All she could think of to say was, 'Then Lily was very lucky to have such a caring big sister,' and hope that her words would convey an intimation of praise.

When Daisy was showing signs of being ready for sleep, Bea left her in Nanny Adams's care and took the girls back to the schoolroom. She set them to draw a picture of spring and write about what they liked best about the season, leaving herself free to wipe down some of the splashes of paint from the wall. She was standing on a chair, her arm stretched out, when the schoolroom door opened and she heard the girls chorus behind her, 'Good morning, Uncle Henry!' as they rose to their feet.

'Oh, my goodness!' Bea exclaimed, wobbling alarmingly. She regained her balance and hastily stepped down from the chair, echoing the girls' greeting.

Henry frowned as he advanced further into the room. 'Good morning, girls, Miss Rossall.' He waved a hand at his nieces. 'Sit down and resume your work, girls.' He was impressed by the quiet industry of the girls – but not so impressed to see their governess balancing precariously on the chair, a wet cloth in her hand. He hadn't expected to see Miss Rossall doing the cleaning herself.

'Should you be doing that, Miss Rossall?' he enquired. 'I thought I had said that my nieces should clean up the mess they made.'

'As indeed they have, Mr Dearden,' she agreed, sweeping her arm around the room. 'See what a good job they have made of it!' Before he could think of a suitable comment, she continued brightly, 'I felt it would not be safe to expect the girls to climb on to a chair to wash the wall, in case they were to fall.'

'Really! Whereas it is perfectly safe for you, Miss Rossall?' he observed sardonically.

'Safe enough, Mr Dearden! Do not fear that I will risk falling off the chair and breaking my legs, thus depriving you of yet another governess.'

There was a glint in her eyes that seemed to challenge him further and he felt a surge of admiration that the hardships of her upbringing had not left her cowed or subservient. He found that she aroused his curiosity. Would her self-possession and strength of character make a difference to the education of his nieces? He hoped so. They needed *something* to dispel the grief and emptiness in their young lives that the loss of their parents had caused.

He glanced around. The room did seem to be tidy once more. 'Yes. Good work,' he murmured, feeling that the evident improvement wrong-footed him in some way. He couldn't help remarking, 'However, it is a bit chilly in here. Shouldn't you have the fire burning more brightly?'

Bea flushed at his criticism. 'I have used all the coals that were in place,' she defended herself. 'I ... wasn't sure that I could ask for more.'

He frowned. 'You needn't be so frugal. I am not short of money!'

His tone was edged with sharpness and Bea sensed that he felt a slur on his generosity of spirit and simply replied, 'No, I realize that – but the fire was kept low yesterday. I thought that was how you preferred it to be.'

'I appreciate your thrift – but do not feel compelled to exercise it to the point of discomfort – neither for yourself nor my nieces. And do not carry the coals upstairs yourself. You must tell Gertie when you need more. She will bring them.'

Bea glanced at him sharply – for she *had* intended to go down for the coals herself! She wasn't used to telling servants to do jobs for her. However, she knew it was part of her new role. 'Thank you. May I also do what I can to brighten up the room? I always feel that children learn better in a pleasant environment, don't you?'

He glanced around. The room was quite bare. Why had he never before noticed its spartan condition? 'You may do whatever you feel necessary, Miss Rossall – within reason, of course. Do you have everything you need with regard to educating my nieces? The previous governesses seemed to bring certain teaching aids with them, whereas I realize that you had no opportunity to do so.'

'Oh!'

He saw the expression of surprise give way to an air of consideration, as she laid the index finger of her right hand against her cheek whilst she thought about his question.

'There seems to be a decided shortage of history, geography and mathematical textbooks,' she mused aloud. 'And other things, such as a globe and anything to encourage an enquiring mind into the wonders of science; not even a magnifying glass!'

He raised an enquiring eyebrow. 'Ah, yes. The tools of your own unconventional education, no doubt? Or is it that there are sewing needles and threads a-plenty and thus of no need of mention?'

'No, there aren't any of those, either but they are probably more easily obtainable from local shops,' she replied, undaunted by his manner.

He inclined his head, indicating that he agreed with her reasoning. He was beginning to realize that her natural pleasantness and underlying sense of humour made the strict formality of other governesses seem stilted by comparison. 'You may inspect my library, Miss Rossall,' he found himself offering, 'and select from it any books you think might be of use to you.'

Her interest was instantly aroused. 'You have a library?'

'Only a moderate one, though there is a selection of encyclopaedias; a number of history and geography books; also atlases and books on travel, science and mathematics.'

Bea beamed her approval. 'And primers and children's novels?' she asked eagerly.

He raised an eyebrow, realizing for some unknown reason that he felt inclined to tease her. 'No primers,' he acknowledged, 'But *novels*, Miss Rossall? Will they not be to the detriment of serious learning?'

'Indeed not!' she replied indignantly. 'I am thinking of such authors as Charles Dickens, Lewis Carroll, Robert Louis Stephenson and Walter Scott. All of whom I am sure you read in your youth.'

'Indeed I did. But you mention no female authors. Are they not to be recommended?'

She smiled briefly in response and he was surprised to feel a lurch somewhere in his midriff. Now, why was that? He knew prettier women who left his emotions unmoved. He realized that Miss Rossall was responding to his teasing riposte.

'Miss Jane Austen's books are highly regarded in many circles, Mr Dearden. As are those of Mrs Gaskell, the Brontë sisters and many other authoresses of renown,' she countered, adding with a gleam in her eyes, '... and you must surely be aware that George Eliot was, in truth, Mary Ann Evans?'

'*Touché*, Miss Rossall! And did your reverend father allow

you to read such popular literature? Was he not afraid that it might contaminate your mind?'

'Indeed not! My father was of the opinion that good choices could only be made if one was given the opportunities to make fair judgements.'

Henry felt, quite rightly, rebuked, but he merely raised his eyebrows, accompanied by a slight nod of acceptance. Good heavens, he had welcomed quite a virago into his home! He could almost imagine her standing alongside Keir Hardie, the outspoken proponent of a political party for the working class, eloquently proclaiming her cause! He wasn't sure whether he ought to be happy or filled with concern.

A sidelong glance towards Winifred and Lily, both of whom were listening to their exchange with open mouths, brought him back to his senses. What *was* he thinking of, engaging their governess in such a discourse? And enjoying it, he reflected wryly. In order to cover his momentary confusion, he took out his fob watch and glanced at the time. 'Make a list of any books that you borrow, Miss Rossall, and another list of anything else you require – and I will consider your requests.' Now, why had he come to the schoolroom? Ah, yes! 'My nieces' letters of apology to Miss Winstanley? They are completed?'

Miss Rossall reached behind him and picked them up from her desk. A faint fragrance of some floral scent wafted past him. It reminded him of a summer's day in the countryside – a picnic in a meadow, he thought. He immediately rejected the thought; he wasn't usually inclined to such poetic musings. Besides, he had work to do. He took the letters from her and glanced at them briefly. 'They seem fine,' he said brusquely. 'I will see that they are posted as soon as possible.'

He included them all in his nod of farewell and left the

schoolroom wondering if the well-ordered pattern of life that he had cultivated around himself was under attack? He hoped not.

On re-entering his study he laughed at his musings. What nonsense! His nieces had been with him for nine or ten months and, apart from the disruption of having to engage a succession of governesses, his life had continued in more or less the same fashion as before. No, the only change was going to be that Miss Rossall had the right spirit – and the energy and vitality – to deal pleasantly and decisively with his two nieces without frequent discourse with him. His life would once more regain the professional aloofness that he preferred.

In the schoolroom there was a visible relaxing of tension when Mr Dearden had made his departure. Bea felt a strange mixture of elation and disquiet coursing though her. Her papa had always encouraged her to question the status quo and discuss current issues, resulting in many a lively debate – but, in her new role, it was probably totally inappropriate. Governesses had to know their place. And, that place, although above other household servants, was certainly not on a par with the master of the house!

She swiftly brought her thoughts under control. 'Carry on with your work, girls. I will soon have this wall clean and before we know it, it will be time for lunch.' She proceeded to dispel any remnants of disquiet within her heart with a show of energetic, physical action.

Later, when she collected the girls' work, she sensed an entirely different feeling of disquiet. Whereas Lily's offering was a drawing of colourful flowers and a few descriptive words, Winifred had written, '*I do not like spring. Winter is best. Winter is cold and dark. Winter is safe.*' And her drawing, originally of some well-defined flowers, was crayoned over in black.

She flickered a glance at Winifred, wondering whether the girl was throwing her a challenge; wanting to draw her into a futile discussion or even a reprimand? But Winifred was studiously ignoring her as she busied herself in gathering together the crayons she had used. Bea felt her heart twist in empathy at the pain the girl must be enduring – a pain that wouldn't be alleviated by hastily expressed sympathy.

A more disturbing symptom of that pain was displayed later that day. They had had lunch in the kitchen, once more under Mrs Kellett's disapproving eye, and had then returned upstairs to the nursery. Bea decided to let Winifred and Lily spend an hour or so playing in the nursery since it was Saturday afternoon. Winifred chose to play with her doll's house again and Lily wanted to play at 'babies' with her newly returned doll.

'But I need some napkins so that I can change her after I've fed her,' Lily requested.

'We could make some,' Bea offered. 'Are there any bits of old towelling anywhere, Nanny Adams?'

'I'm sure I can find something, my dear. I'll have a look in my mending box and why don't you have a look in the linen cupboard? I'm sure I've seen a pile of old flannelette sheets too. They could be cut down to size for Daisy.'

Nanny Adams went into the small bedroom and, with both girls playing happily, Bea left the nursery and went into the bathroom just across the way. She quickly found the pile of old sheets and some frayed towels, too. She had just selected one of each when she heard Lily say, 'What are you doing, Winnie? You know we haven't to go near the fire.'

Bea quickly replaced the unwanted items and hurried back to the nursery. Winifred was leaning over the fireguard and something was burning brightly among the coals.

'What have you put on the fire, Winifred?' Bea asked sharply.

Winifred whirled round, her face showing guilt. 'Nothing,' she replied. 'It was just some rubbish.'

'Now, you know you've not to do that, Miss Winnie.' Nanny Adams was back in the room. She went across to the fire and poked at the coals. 'Eh, Miss Winnie!' She glanced at Bea but only shook her head and pressed her lips together. 'Well, don't do it again, Miss Winnie,' she reproved the child.

'What has Winifred burned?' Bea asked curiously.

Nanny Adams glanced at Winifred and then shook her head. 'It was just some old bits and pieces,' she said, shrugging slightly.

Winifred tossed her head back, her face portraying some satisfaction at Nanny Adams's backing of her. Bea felt puzzled. She suspected it had been a bit more than 'bits and pieces' but felt she couldn't contradict Nanny Adams's assessment of what it had been. She had to let it go.

Later, when she was on her own in the day room, she discovered what had been burned. Daisy was settled in her makeshift cot in Bea's bedroom and Nanny Adams was overseeing the girls' bedtime bath. Under Bea's insistence the girls had tidied their toys away but she was idly tidying the room in general, in the belief that a tidy environment encouraged tidy minds.

The wooden box that held the toy figures was on the floor behind one of the easy chairs. She bent down to pick it up. It felt different. She gently shook it and then opened the lid. As she suspected, the box was empty. A frown creased her forehead as she glanced around but there was no sign of the three figures.

With a sinking heart, she knew that Winifred was so determined not to give them a place in her life that she had thrown them on to the fire.

Chapter 8

SUNDAY DAWNED WITH a lively breeze blowing away the few remaining clouds scudding across a clear blue sky. Knowing that she would be expected to accompany Mr Dearden and his nieces to church, Bea delegated the care of Daisy to Nanny Adams.

Neither Winifred nor Lily was making any effort to get her coat on.

'Come along, girls!' Bea encouraged them. 'Your uncle will be wondering what is keeping us if we don't get a move on!'

'We aren't going to church this morning!' Winifred announced defiantly.

'Oh? And whose decision is that?'

'Mine – and Lily's!'

'I think your uncle will override that decision,' Bea responded.

Winifred folded her arms across her chest. 'He can't make us! We'll scream all the way there! Church is boring. So, we aren't going, are we, Lily?' When Lily didn't reply, Winifred nudged her with her elbow. '*Are* we?' she insisted.

'No,' Lily muttered, hanging her head.

Bea considered the rebellious pair. 'Hmm! I can remember what happened when I once decided not to go to church,' she reminisced, with a faint smile.

Winifred scowled at her but Lily looked interested. 'What happened?' she asked.

'My mother told me that I would have to sit quietly in the kitchen with my arms folded during the whole morning – and also for an equal length of time in the afternoon. It was a lovely day. The sun was shining, just as it is today, and I wanted to go out to play in the afternoon, so I decided it would be better to go to church and have my afternoon free.'

'Huh! I don't believe you!' Winifred declared, thudding her folded arms at her chest once more.

Bea smiled gently. 'I can truthfully assure you, Winifred, that I never tell a deliberate lie.'

'Never?' Lily asked in awed tones.

'It's never worth it. You feel bad inside.'

'I don't!' Winifred contradicted her. 'I like telling lies!'

'Do you like it when others tell lies to you, Winifred?'

Winifred's eyes narrowed, sensing a trap. She eventually thrust her chin forward. 'I don't care! Grown ups always tell lies to children. They think we don't know – but we do!'

Bea laid a hand gently on Winifred's shoulder. 'Winifred, I promise you now, I will always tell you the truth. And, as we have little time left to get ready for church, I assure you I will carry out what my mother threatened if you don't begin to get ready immediately.' She paused, considering whether a bit of bribery might be judicious at this point. She decided it was and continued, 'And what I *would* like us to do this afternoon is to ask Mrs Kellett for some biscuits and a bottle of lemonade and go for a walk somewhere. I have no idea where, because I have only just come to Horwich, but I will ask your uncle and I'm sure he knows somewhere where we could go on such a sunny Sunday afternoon.'

Winifred obstinately pursed her lips but Lily tugged at her

arm. 'It would be nice, Winnie!' she pleaded. 'Uncle Henry might say we can go up that lane to the top of the Pike. He said he used to fly a kite up there. Maybe he'll make one for us if we are good?'

Bea could see that Winifred was weakening and decided to make it easier for her. 'I'll leave you to make up your minds, girls. I am going along to my room to put my coat on. If you decide you are coming to church, you may meet me at the top of the stairs in five minutes' time. Otherwise, you must go and sit in the schoolroom until we return and I will alert Nanny Adams to the fact that that is where she will find you after she has settled Daisy.'

She left them to think it over, wondering just how she would resolve it if Winifred held firm. She couldn't imagine Mr Dearden dragging a screaming child along to church.

Bea's heart sank when she emerged from her room. Only Lily was waiting at the top of the stairs. 'Where's Winifred?' she asked as casually as she could manage.

Lily's eyes slid sideways. 'It's all right. She's … er … coming. She just had to … er … get something from the kitchen. She said she'll meet us in the hall.'

'Oh. What did she need to get?'

'Er … a clean hankie, I think she said.'

Bea raised an eyebrow. Lily's cheeks flushed with a pink hue but, at that moment, Winifred appeared at the foot of the stairs, just as Mr Dearden emerged from his study, looking at his fob watch.

'Come along, Lily. Let's join your sister and your uncle,' Bea said briskly, leading the way down the stairs. 'I hope we haven't kept you waiting, Mr Dearden.'

'Only a little.' He opened the front door and allowed them to pass through before him down the steps and on to the path that led to Chorley Old Road. 'However, we do need to walk briskly, so don't dawdle, girls!'

'No, Uncle Henry,' the girls chorused, falling into step just behind him. Bea wasn't sure whom she should be walking with but, as the girls, heads close as they giggled about something, dropped a few steps behind, she found herself alongside Mr Dearden.

What a difference a bit of sunshine made! Her heart felt quite light and she was filled with optimism that things were going to work out well after all. She glanced around as they walked. 'Oh! There are hills! And is that a castle I can see?'

'It is called Rockhaven Castle ... although it's not a castle in the real sense of the word. Just a private residence with castellated walls. And, further to the left, that's Rivington Pike. The watchtower on the top dates from the days of the Spanish Armada.'

'And a good place to fly to a kite,' Bea murmured, remembering Lily's comment.

She was rewarded by a quizzical raising of Mr Dearden's eyebrow, a quirk of his that Bea was already learning to expect.

'Something the girls mentioned,' she said smiling. 'I've never flown a kite.'

'Then that is something we can easily rectify one day,' Mr Dearden promised, remembering vaguely that he had made a similar promise to his nieces a good while ago. Pressure of work had driven it from his mind. He frowned. What was it about Miss Rossall that made him volunteer to give up some of his time?

As they turned in through the gate of Holy Trinity Church they joined other parishioners who were walking up the short path to the main door. A well-dressed middle-aged couple made a point of greeting Mr Dearden and they all paused whilst Mr

Dearden responded to the greeting. A fashionably dressed young lady who accompanied them, presumably their daughter, laid a hand on Mr Dearden's arm.

'We missed you at the Conservative Club meeting last evening, Mr Dearden – and at the social event afterwards.' She pouted coyly. 'I thought I had persuaded you to attend.'

Mr Dearden inclined his head. 'I'm sorry if I gave you the impression that I might attend, Miss Hawsley. As you know, I have the responsibility of my two young nieces at present and I cannot always plan ahead.' In truth, he had completely forgotten the invitation. Dismayed by his social indiscretion, he turned to indicate Miss Rossall and unwittingly made another. 'May I introduce Miss Rossall, my nieces' new governess? Miss Rossall, Mr and Mrs Hawsley and Miss Hawsley.'

Bea smiled – but faltered when it was obvious that none of the trio thought fit to smile in return. Mr and Mrs Hawsley barely flicked their eyes in her direction. Miss Hawsley threw her a haughty glance, eyeing her from head to foot, but swiftly returned her full attention to Mr Dearden. Her lips curled disparagingly.

'Another governess, Mr Dearden? However, I cannot pretend to be surprised. I thought the previous one to be rather over-strung. Did you forget my recommendation of Miss Pilling, should you be disappointed yet again? She is renowned for her excellent discipline. It's not too late to change your mind. I could telegraph her tomorrow.'

'Thank you – but, no, Miss Hawsley. The situation required an immediate solution and Miss Rossall has agreed to a month's trial. I am sure things will work out satisfactorily.'

Miss Hawsley's faint, 'Hmph!' was almost drowned out by her mother's sharp, 'I hope you won't disappoint us by forgoing our invitation to dinner on Tuesday, Mr Dearden? And, afterwards, we have tickets for the Choral Society's concert at the Mechanics' Institute.'

Mr Dearden bowed his head. 'Of course. I am looking forward to it.'

'Good!' Mr Hawsley responded curtly. 'Shall we proceed into church?' He offered his arm to Mrs Hawsley and Miss Hawsley took possession of Mr Dearden's left arm, leaving Bea to follow on behind with Winifred and Lily. She wondered whether Miss Hawsley were the particular friend Mrs Kellett had referred to, and would they now all sit together?

'I told you Miss Horseface doesn't like us!' Winifred whispered to Lily as they entered the magnificent high-vaulted nave of Holy Trinity church. Lily giggled.

'Quiet, girls!' Bea reprimanded them, not totally sure that she had heard aright.

The Hawsleys entered a boxed pew on the right, six rows from the front, and Bea was relieved when Mr Dearden ushered his party to the opposite pew on the left, thankful to be distanced from the Hawsleys.

During the second hymn a sudden squeal from a girl in the pew in front of them caused consternation amongst the nearby congregation. The girl began to shriek and jump from foot to foot, clinging to her mama's arm. 'A mouse, Mama! It's a mouse!'

The interest rippled outwards, drawing curious gazes.

'Hush, dear! People are looking!' the girl's mama hissed, her face flushing at being the centre of such a commotion.

'Ooh!' Undeterred, the young lady leaped on to the wooden seat, shaking her skirt and squealing even more loudly. The girl's father, a well-dressed man of severe expression, started to beat about the floor with his hymn book upon which his wife hurriedly scrambled on to the pew to join her daughter, shaking her skirt and adding *her* squeals to the commotion.

The singing faltered and gradually came to a ragged stop, leaving only the organist playing on regardless. Winifred and Lily fell into each other's arm, smothering hysterical laughter against each other's coat.

'Restrain yourselves, girls!' Bea hissed at them, her face reddening, knowing that all eyes were focusing in the direction of the two pews. The girls made an effort to obey her injunction but failed to maintain it. They sank on to their seat and collapsed into a heap of choked laughter.

Mr Dearden threw them a thunderous glance – then stepped out of his pew and opened the door of the one in front. 'Allow me, Mr Greenhalgh. Oh!' He stepped aside hastily.

'It *is* a mouse, Mama! See! There it goes!' a young boy shrieked, causing worshippers across the aisle to crane their necks forward. They moved their heads in unison as they followed the mouse's progress towards the Reverend Pigot. With great presence of mind, the Reverend Pigot lifted his vestments as the mouse reached him, allowing the small creature to pass unheeded into hiding behind the altar.

'Pray, don't be alarmed, ma'am. The mouse has gone,' Bea said soothingly to the highly discomfited woman in front of her who was now making an undignified descent from the seat.

'Take us home at once, Mr Greenhalgh!' the woman demanded of her husband.

'Do get down, Eliza – and stop that noise at once! We are leaving!' Mr Greenhalgh snapped at his daughter. He glared at the occupants of the Deardens' pew as he hustled his wife and daughter into the aisle. Mrs Greenhalgh, red of face, held her head high as she swept down to the rear door, her eyes fixed straight ahead, dragging the still-sobbing Eliza with her.

Bea felt somehow responsible – but she had been taken completely by surprise. Where had Winifred got a mouse from at such short notice? Had she carried it to church in her pocket? No wonder the girls had been whispering and giggling so much!

'Pick up your hymn books and, Winifred, stand on my other side!' she bade them grimly, regarding them sternly as they obeyed her command. 'I will speak to you at home.'

The congregation gradually realized that the impromptu show was over and joined in the last verse of 'O worship the King, all-glorious above'. Bea resolutely sang out as lustily as she was able, thankful that she knew the words so well, since the out-of-focus words danced around the page of her hymn book. She fixed her eyes on a point above the Reverend Pigot's head, hoping that Mr Dearden's mercies would be as tender as God's – because she was certain that he knew as well as she how the mouse had come to be released into the pew in front of them.

At the end of the service Mr Dearden strode out of church immediately behind the Reverend Pigot and the choir, not waiting for the dignitaries in the front pews to proceed before him. Bea placed herself firmly between the two girls and hurried in his wake along the path towards the gate. At least their hasty departure prevented any further conversation with the Hawsleys.

None of the party spoke a word during the short journey home. Bea hoped Mr Dearden would leave it to her to question the girls and impose whatever punishment she felt to be fitting. It wasn't to be. As he unlocked the front door and stood aside to allow them entry into the house, he said, 'I will speak to you girls in my study. You as well, Miss Rossall.'

Bea's heart sank as they passed in front of him. She didn't

know him well enough to know whether he were truly angry –
or was about to make a token reprimand. She stood at his side,
facing the girls. Lily hung her head but Winifred tilted up her
chin and stared defiantly ahead.

'Well? What have you to say?' Mr Dearden demanded.

'What about, Uncle Henry?' Winifred asked boldly.

'You know very well "what about", young lady! I wasn't born
yesterday!' He turned to Lily, an easier quarry. 'Lily? What was
your part in releasing that mouse during the service?'

Lily glanced anxiously at her sister – but Winifred stared
straight ahead.

'Well, I … that is, Winnie said …'

'Sneak!' Winifred hissed, now glaring down at Lily. 'I told you
not to say anything!'

Lily bit her lip, looking close to tears. 'I haven't – I won't,' she
stammered, too late now for her denial to be of use.

'Winifred?' Mr Dearden asked calmly, his eyebrow raised as
he swung back to the elder girl.

Winifred, no coward, flung back her hair. 'I thought it would
liven up the service.'

Bea had to suck in her cheeks to prevent her lips twitching
into a smile. It had certainly done that!

Mr Dearden, however, was not amused. 'You gave no
thought to the feelings of Mrs Greenhalgh and her daughter.
Nor of anyone else who might have been affected. Mrs
Greenhalgh was humiliated at being made such a public spec-
tacle! Well, your escapade will not go unpunished. You will go
straight to the schoolroom and remain there all afternoon. I
will instruct Mrs Kellett to serve you a plain lunch. Miss
Rossall, you will decide how to occupy my nieces – and I trust
you will not be too lenient!'

'But we are going out for a picnic!' Winifred protested. 'Miss

Rossall promised!' She turned on Bea. 'You lied!' she spat at her. 'You said you never tell lies – but you did!'

'I didn't lie, Winifred,' Bea reproved her gently. 'I fully intended to take you out, but your behaviour merits a punishment and your uncle has decided you cannot go out this afternoon.'

'It makes no difference! You promised you would take us out and now you're not going to! You've broken your word! I'll never believe you again!' On that defiant note, Winifred rushed out of the room and let the door slam behind her.

Mr Dearden strode to the door and yanked it open. 'Winifred! Come back here at once! I will not allow you to speak in such a way!' But Winifred's fleeing steps didn't even pause. He turned back to face Bea. 'Well, Miss Rossall? My nieces were in your charge. What have you to say?'

Her cheeks flushed at his criticism and she looked quite uncomfortable. He felt a sudden desire to assure her that he hadn't meant his remark as a personal attack but restrained the impulse. His life was complicated enough at present.

Besides, Miss Rossall took a step back, a glint of fire in her eyes. 'I obviously underestimated Winifred's ability to create a diversion!' She paused for a moment, her expression suddenly curious. 'But I wonder how she managed to acquire a mouse so readily?'

He felt his anger dispersing and twisted his lips wryly. 'She probably had it in readiness in order to torment Miss Winstanley. She has done it before. So be warned, Miss Rossall. And do not be too trusting in future.'

After Miss Rossall and Lily had followed Winifred upstairs, Henry reflected that it wasn't the first time a church service had been disrupted by a deliberately released rodent – except that Freddie's released captive had been a large rat! He laughed out loud at the memory. Now *that* had caused almost the whole congregation to leap on to their pews!

Chapter 9

BEA SPENT THE next few days getting to know what the girls could do academically. It was no surprise to discover that they were stilted in presenting their learning. Consequently, she determined to let her own imagination run riot as she planned their lessons.

Instead of history being a list of dates, she developed a plan to help the girls find out how the historical events and great inventions of the past century had led to great changes in the everyday life of all classes of the population – the emergence of gas lighting; water supplies being piped into individual houses; the railways carrying fresh foods and manufactured goods from one end of the country to the other. She was sure all of this would be reflected in the growing town of Horwich.

She would take them on discovery trips around the town. Identifying new buildings and writing down accounts of what they had discovered, accompanied by drawings, would enrich both their use of language and artistic skills; looking in shop windows and noting the prices of goods for sale would make use of their arithmetical skills; and the scientific developments would be researched in order to evaluate their benefits to the general population in medical and practical uses. There was no end to her ideas. She hoped Mr Dearden would approve of them.

She laid them before him early on Wednesday evening when she went to ask whether the time was convenient for her to look through his library to find any books that she might find useful.

'Of course,' he agreed at once. 'If you are willing to wait until after dinner, Miss Rossall, I will be happy to help you find some useful books. Let me see …' He pulled out his watch to check the time. 'I am due to dine in about ten minutes. It will probably save time if you dine with me tonight – and you can tell me more about these proposals as we eat.'

Bea looked at him in some consternation. She didn't want to socialize with her employer. It might lead to unwelcome complications. She pushed her spectacles firmly to the bridge of her nose 'I have had tea with Winifred and Lily,' she hastened to explain. 'And I'm not dressed. Besides, I don't want to make extra work for Mrs Kellett.'

'Tea? Nursery tea? Is that all you have?'

'Well, yes … but it is quite adequate, I assure you.'

'Indeed it is not!' Mr Dearden said in exasperation. He wondered why he hadn't thought of it before. Though, on reflection, not one of his nieces' previous governesses had ever piqued his interest as much as Miss Rossall did. He had found their maidenly ways quite irritating. Now, he found himself enthused by the idea of Miss Rossall dining with him. He declared quite firmly, 'You will dine with me every evening from now on. I assure you, it is quite proper. Your position in this household is not that of a servant. You are the daughter of a clergyman and are here as governess. And don't look so alarmed! There are no other guests invited to dine with me tonight! And even if there were, no one would think that there was anything amiss.'

Bea's right hand fluttered at her throat. She could think of least one of his friends who might find the idea of her dining with Mr Dearden too forward a presumption! Besides, wasn't this the very reason why she had made her appearance more severe? She would rather tuck herself away upstairs once her daily duties were over.

Or would she? Her sudden doubt stilled her agitation. Did she really enjoy her solitary mealtimes? She missed her father's wide range of conversational topics and she was beginning to look forward to the occasions when her employer took an interest in his nieces' progress.

And he had only asked her to *dine* with him, for heaven's sake! What harm was there in *that*? It would remain as formal an event as they chose to make it – and some intelligent adult company would most certainly be welcome. Even so, the idea of having to spend part of each evening with Mr Dearden made her feel quite nervous. It really wasn't a good idea. She was sure Mrs Kellett would think it highly presumptuous of her, too.

'But I haven't settled Daisy yet, Mr Dearden,' she faltered, seeking a reasonable excuse that wouldn't imply ingratitude.

'I am sure Nanny Adams is only too pleased to take Daisy under her wing – and it will give you a regular opportunity to bring me up to date with what you have achieved with my nieces. I am interested in your methods of educating them. So, run upstairs and change and I will go to the kitchen to inform Mrs Kellett of our new arrangement.' Mr Dearden looked pleased with himself. 'Shall we say … in fifteen minutes?'

Bea could see no way out. 'Very well,' she murmured and hurried upstairs, not totally sure the right decision had been made. Her heart fluttered in agitation. What if he turned out to be like Cyril Ackroyd? No, surely not. She was doing him a great disservice even to contemplate that he might put her character at risk as Mr Ackroyd had done – and tonight's aim was purely to discuss which reference books would be the most suitable ones for her to borrow. That was all. She would present a calm, professional front and make sure that any responses she made could be in no way misinterpreted.

As he watched her fleeing figure, Henry also suffered momentary misgivings – which he quelled impatiently. It would be a daily opportunity to check on his nieces' progress under Miss Rossall's tutelage. Though, if he were to be totally honest, the sounds of laughter he heard emanating from the schoolroom and the day nursery on occasions, a phenomenon that had never occurred under the rule of any of the previous governesses, often aroused his curiosity and he had found himself to be listening out for such sounds whilst working at home the past three days.

In the kitchen, he sensed Mrs Kellett's disapproval of his revised dining plan but refused to be deterred by it. He was the master here – and weren't things changing throughout society? It was an era of change! The fact that a woman could be educated to the standard Miss Rossall had achieved showed that.

Of course, there were limits to the role of women in society. A man must always be in the position of authority over the women of his household, even though Miss Rossall seemed to suggest that that line of thinking was somewhat outdated. Hmm, the evening promised to be a stimulating occasion. He was looking forward to it.

Stimulating and eye-opening was Henry's opinion by the time he bade Miss Rossall goodnight. What a difference from his dinner with the Hawsleys the previous evening! There, the conversation over dinner had been on superficial matters, generally concerning what Mr Hawsley regarded as suitable for the ladies – and none of them had objected. It was only after the ladies withdrew that more 'manly' topics were aired and expounded. Henry smiled to himself, wondering what Mr Hawsley would think if he had been present at his dinner table this evening. Somehow, he felt the older man would have been scandalized.

Without raising her voice or attempting to overstate her points of view, Miss Rossall had challenged the basis of his thinking – and his mind reeled with visions of a future for society as Miss Rossell saw it. Why, if Miss Rossall's thoughts were replicated by women in general, not only would it be possible for women to enter universities and study the same courses as their male counterparts as they now did, but they might also be awarded *degrees*! And not degrees of a lower level, as he had tried to advocate. Oh, no! Miss Rossall insisted that she would be satisfied with nothing less than an equal standard.

Further discussion had elicited the aspiration that at some point in the not-too-distant future, women would be allowed to vote for their parliamentary representative. Yet, if that were to happen, sooner or later some misguided female might have the temerity to stand for parliament herself. Now *that* he had felt justified in decrying!

Of course, Miss Rossall's unsuppressed twinkling of her eyes behind her spectacles showed that she, too, was not *entirely* serious in that last supposition – but he eventually retired to bed with his mind stimulated beyond any recent experience.

That Miss Rossall's thinking process was uncluttered by female whims and fancies was evident from the way she had set out her proposals for the education of his nieces – proposals that held interesting possibilities. He had been happy to give Miss Rossall free rein with her plans and now, as he lay sleepless in his bed, he reflected that he would like to follow her progress with Winifred and Lily more closely. Mmm, maybe he should make it his practice to pay a mid-morning call to the schoolroom? But that wouldn't be until Friday, the day after tomorrow. It was something he found himself looking forward to.

Bea was enjoying her job and the girls were settling into a harmonious routine. There were minor difficulties, mainly with Winifred, but nothing that was insurmountable. She was discovering that the more she challenged the girl's level of intelligence, the more responsive Winifred became. Maybe boredom had played a major role in her rebellious behaviour?

The following afternoon, Thursday, Bea asked the girls what they knew about the town they lived in. They looked at her blankly.

'Well, it's called Horwich,' Winifred began hesitantly.

'And there's lots of streets – long streets of houses, all joined together,' Lily added, 'but they've not got gardens like we have here.'

'And some shops,' Winifred continued, warming to the theme, 'but we've never been in any of them. Miss Winstanley said we would pick up germs.'

'And there's a lot of dirty smoke down there. All the children have dirty faces. I don't think they wash themselves like we do,' Lily opined.

'Maybe not,' Bea agreed. 'Now, I think the best way to learn more about Horwich is to take a walk round the town and find out just what is there.'

'Really?' Winifred asked incredulously. 'Straight away?'

'No, it's too late to go now. What we can do this afternoon is

make a list of things we can look out for. So, if you will each get
a piece of paper and a pencil, I will write your suggestions on
the blackboard and you can copy them down.'

Bea was looking forward to sharing her plans with Mr
Dearden over dinner but had to forgo that pleasure when Mrs
Kellett took great delight in informing her that their employer
had sent a message to say that a problem had occurred at the
Loco Works and he would be eating at the Railway Café with
some colleagues from the drawing office.

'So, yer'll be eatin' on yer own agen tonight, like all t'other
governesses have done!' Mrs Kellett announced, her expression
triumphant.

Bea hoped her disappointment didn't show as she replied
calmly, 'Thank you for letting me know, Mrs Kellett. If you will
put my dinner on to a tray, maybe Gertie will bring it up to my
room when it is ready.'

'Hmph! Getting uppity now, aren't we?' Mrs Kellett's
muttered.

Bea sighed but refused to be downhearted about it. Most
governesses would find the same resentment from the lower
servants and, in her case, it was accentuated by her unconventional hiring.

Soon after ten o'clock on Friday morning Henry was momentarily surprised when, alerted by the sound of female chatter
outside his study, he discovered that Miss Rossall, carrying
Daisy in a sling made out of a shawl, was ushering his nieces
through the front door. His next reaction was one of disappointment.

'Oh, are you going out, Miss Rossall? I had intended to join
you in the schoolroom for some time this morning.' Miss
Rossall seemed a little taken aback and he added swiftly, 'To

make myself more familiar with your methods of teaching – nothing in the way of being critical or disapproving, I assure you.'

Her face relaxed. 'That is your prerogative as my employer, Mr Dearden. Do you wish me to change our plans and have an indoor lesson?'

He followed her glance at his nieces and saw their lively expressions cloud over. He recalled a comment Miss Hawsley had made during dinner on Tuesday, warning him that Miss Rossall would take advantage of his good nature. He was now torn between heeding her advice or trusting Miss Rossall's judgement.

His dilemma was solved when Miss Rossall added, 'We are going on an educational exploratory tour of Horwich town centre. We will draw a map of our excursion on our return and draw in any buildings that we notice. At some future date, I intend to discover which buildings have been erected during the nineteenth century, so that we can see how the town has grown in recent years, especially since the locomotive works came to Horwich.'

Ah, he should have known this wasn't a simple pleasure excursion. 'I think I can help you with that, Miss Rossall. Somewhere in the office at the loco works, I am sure there are some mapped drawings of the town, done by the original surveyors when the management of the Lancashire and Yorkshire Railway Company decided to move the works to Horwich. I will look them out for you, so that you and the girls can see where changes have been made.' He was about to return to his study but paused to ask, 'But, tell me, Miss Rossall, why are you carrying Daisy in a sling made out of a shawl? Surely, her weight will make you tired very quickly. Could she not be left in the care of Nanny Adams?'

'Nanny Adams is full of a cold today and I didn't wish to impose upon her,' Bea replied. 'Besides, Daisy is used to it. It's one of the age-old ways that working mothers have used to cope with caring for their children.'

'But not, generally, governesses.'

He saw his reproof had hit home – but, before she had time to frame a response, a resolution to the problem occurred to him. 'I am sure that our old perambulator is still up in the attic,' he mused. 'Yes, I'm sure it is. I'll send Gertie up to take a look.'

'Oh!'

She looked taken aback – and he could tell she was going to protest. Another idea came to him. 'In fact, even better – we can all go up together tomorrow morning and have a treasure hunt. You can incorporate it into your project. After all, if the perambulator is there, it must be about thirty-three years old and as much a part of history as I am.'

He saw his nieces smile at that and felt inordinately pleased that he had amused them. 'So, that's settled, then. It will be a fitting end to your first week here. Are we agreed?'

He knew he had won from the way Miss Rossall's features relaxed, and he felt a tingle of pleasure at the knowledge that he was beginning to read her facial expressions. She really was the most surprising creature, he thought benignly – a curious mixture of being a forward thinker, yet somehow, as shown by the severity of her appearance, still conforming to the outlook of the present century. Almost like a butterfly hesitating to emerge from its chrysalis, he mused.

Bea wanted to refuse, but a glance at Winifred and Lily persuaded her of their hope that she would agree. How could she deny the girls time with their uncle?

'Very well,' she capitulated primly. 'Will half past ten suit you? Daisy is usually settled again by then, should Nanny Adams still be feeling a little under the weather.'

'Half past ten it is,' he agreed. He felt surprisingly light-hearted as he returned to his study. Yes, a morning searching the attic might be just what his nieces needed. He felt a tingle of anticipation. Yes, it was a good idea.

As they started on their walk around town, with Lily chattering about what they might find in the attic, and even Winifred showing some interest, Bea began to feel an air of anticipation herself. There had never been anything to store in the attic at home, since her parents gave everything away to those poorer than themselves. What would they find?

Their town-discovery expedition was far more successful than Bea had dared hope and her enthusiastic recounting of it ensured a lively discussion over dinner that evening. Henry felt strangely disappointed when Miss Rossall rose from her seat at the end of the meal, declaring her intention to retire, but his offer to withdraw for coffee was politely turned down.

'I have Daisy to feed and coffee drunk too late seems to enliven my brain too much,' she declined with a smile.

Henry bowed his assent. 'Until tomorrow morning, then.'

Bea took her leave, aware that she would have enjoyed staying longer in Mr Dearden's company, but she dared not. She enjoyed their conversations too much, especially the verbal sparring that frequently took place. It was difficult to restrain her animation when discussing topics close to her heart – indeed, she knew she often failed to keep her enthusiasm in check. She was in danger of encouraging too relaxed a relationship with her employer than was seemly. She mustn't allow it to happen. It could bring about her dismissal ... and that was too dreadful a thought to entertain.

*

The girls were too excited to eat their breakfast properly and were in danger of provoking their governess's patience to its limit. Even their Uncle Henry seemed as happy as a schoolboy as he led the way up the narrow staircase, holding a closed lantern aloft. Once they were in the attic, they delved into the haphazard disarray. They found a box of toys, containing a trumpet and a drum, a set of skittles and a bag of marbles; a box of farm animals and a wooden farm set on a large board with some cowsheds and other buildings on it. Bea felt a degree of contentment as she heard Winifred's voice declaring various finds, feeling that the girl was enjoying the task.

The perambulator was discovered, stacked high with other items, and Bea concentrated on helping Mr Dearden empty its contents, so that it could be pulled out towards the door.

'That was our cricket set,' Henry said as she lifted up a bundle of thick sticks. 'Do girls play cricket?'

'I don't see why not!' Bea laughed, 'though I'm not sure how to play it properly.'

'Then I can see I will have to teach you all,' Henry offered, much to his own surprise. 'There should be a football somewhere, as well. I bet the city boys did that!'

'You're right. They used to chalk the goal posts on the ends of a building or use their rolled-up pullovers to mark out the goal space. I remember once being very cross because they used my rag doll and she got trampled on! But they had to make do with kicking a ball of rags instead of a proper ball.'

'Why was that?' Winifred asked curiously.

'Because everyone where I lived was very poor,' Bea said lightly. 'There was never enough money to buy toys, so we all made our own. It's surprising what you can do when the need arises. In fact, that would make a good topic to think about in our project, wouldn't it? So I'll say no more about what we used to do, then you will have to think for yourselves.'

'And here's a cradle!' Lily cried, trying to tug it out from under some boxes, which then tumbled to the floor, raising a cloud of dust. 'That will be better for Daisy, won't it, Miss Rossall?'

That was the last big 'find' and Henry promised to ask Gregson to help him to get the large things down from the attic that afternoon, ready to be scrubbed clean in the yard. As he scrubbed himself clean in the bathroom, he found himself humming a popular air, a thing he rarely did. When he searched for cause, it came to him that he was enjoying the satisfaction of having spent the morning laughing and getting dirty. He realized, with a start, that he had enjoyed the company of his nieces. Had he settled down into being a staid bachelor far too soon? Or was this just a novelty sensation that might quickly fade?

He knew his thoughts were never far from his nieces' school-room ... nor from their governess, and he was spending more days working at home than he had ever done before. What was he hoping for? He didn't know. In fact, the more he thought about it, the less sure he was. His spirit plummeted.

At that moment he almost wished he could go back to the time before his nieces had invaded his privacy. His life had been uncomplicated. He had been happy and contented, and when they were gone, that was what he would return to. Miss Rossall would leave; she might possibly go with them and become part of Freddie's household.

Somehow, that thought didn't give him the peace of mind he had expected.

Chapter 10

THAT EVENING BEA ate her dinner alone again, as Mr Dearden had been invited to dinner at Ridgmont House, the home of a local business man who owned Wallsuches Bleachworks. She looked forward to a quiet evening. She would have longer to play with Daisy and would be able to oversee her bath-time, allowing Nanny Adams, still in the throes of her cold, to retire early to bed.

Nanny Adams, having hemmed two cot-sheets ready for use, gratefully left Bea in temporary charge of the nursery. As Bea undressed Daisy for her bath, she was surprised to notice tiny bruises on Daisy's arms and legs.

'Now, what's caused those?' she pondered aloud.

Lily cast an anxious glance at her sister.

'Don't look at *me*!' Winifred declared. 'I never hold her.'

Lily's face flared into colour. '*I* haven't hurt her,' she whispered miserably.

Bea hugged her. 'Never mind. It's so easy to bruise babies,' she said gently. 'They have such a delicate skin. Always hold her firmly, supporting her body, not by her arms or legs. See, like this.' She demonstrated her words as she bathed Daisy and dressed her in a clean napkin and flannelette nightgown.

When Daisy's bottle was ready Lily looked wistful. 'Can I still give her her bottle? I will be careful.'

Bea readily assented. 'Yes, of course. I know you'll be careful.' She made sure Lily was seated properly in the chair and placed Daisy in her arms, satisfied that Lily handled Daisy correctly. When she returned from emptying the small bath of its water, she was surprised to find Daisy crying and Lily looking slightly flushed.

'I didn't do anything,' Lily protested. 'She just started to cry.'

Winifred looked smug. 'I told you she wouldn't like you,' she taunted her sister.

Lily looked tearful and Bea hastened to reassure her. 'It's probably a bit of wind in her tummy,' she suggested. 'Here, give her to me for a minute and I'll see if she can burp it up.'

A tiny burp eventually brought a smile to Daisy's face and Bea returned her to Lily's arms for the rest of her bottle. Lily beamed with delight.

Winifred made a face at her. When she realized that Bea had seen her, she declared, 'I'm going to the bathroom,' and flounced out.

Bea sighed. She wished Winifred would accept Daisy into her family circle. Caring for Daisy was helping Lily to cope with the recent changes in her young life; whereas Winifred was holding on to her grief and building resentment against all who wanted to help her. Bea's heart went out to her.

When the baby had been fed and winded again, Bea carried her to her room, meeting Winifred on her way back to the nursery. 'Come and see Daisy in her new cradle,' Bea invited her.

Winifred shrugged her shoulders but turned back and trailed after Bea and Lily.

'Ooh, it's lovely!' Lily cried. 'All it needs is a pretty cover like Nanny Adams knitted for my dolly last Christmas. I'll ask her to make one for Daisy, shall I?'

'That would be nice, Lily,' Bea agreed. 'In fact, I will ask Nanny Adams to show you how to knit and then you can both help? If we all knit some squares, we can sew them together and make a small blanket. How about that?'

Lily bounced on to Bea's bed in excitement. 'Ooh, yes!'

Winifred grabbed hold of her arm and pulled her off the bed. 'Don't do that!' she hissed. 'Come on; let's go back to the nursery.' She pulled Lily out of the room and they ran back to the nursery. Bea shovelled a few coals on to the fire and replaced the small fire-guard before following them. She was planning to have a cosy evening by the fire once the girls were settled.

Later, having made sure Nanny Adams was also settled for the night, Bea ventured downstairs into Mr Dearden's library to choose a novel to read. She chose *Little Dorritt*, as she hadn't read it before, and returned with it to her room. All was quiet and she sighed in contentment. Time to herself until Daisy next awoke – sheer bliss! It had been a busy week, getting used to her new role, but now she was going to relax.

She removed her spectacles and squeezed her eyelids together as she rubbed the heels of her hands against them, easing away the ache and tension. Ah, that was better! She'd been conscious of a slight headache over the past few days and wondered whether her papa's spectacles might be the cause. She planned to find an optician when she received her first wage and hoped to persuade him that she needed a very light prescription for a new pair. Until then, she had to manage as best she could.

She pulled out the pins that held her hair in its tight bun, shaking her hair loose, relishing the sense of freedom as it cascaded down her back. Mmm, better again! She turned up the gaslights, then poked the fire into life. The resulting flames added their dancing sparkle to the room and, with another contented sigh, she settled on her chair by the fire and opened her book. Now for *Little Dorritt*. It began in Marseille in December 1855. Engrossed, she read on....

A small thud as her book hit the carpet jerked Bea awake. She blinked and realized that she had been asleep. The fire was no more than glowing embers and a chill was already settling upon the room. Yawning, she picked up her book and rose to her feet, stretching her arms above her head to ease the aching muscles across her shoulders and the back of her neck. Oh, dear. She hadn't got very far with *Little Dorritt*, had she?

She had no idea what time it was but she guessed it was late. And Daisy hadn't woken for her late-evening feed. She decided to get undressed and go to bed. Daisy's cries would waken her. She placed the bottle of milk in the pan and pushed the trivet over the low embers. All was quiet in the house as she hurried to the bathroom. Back in her room, she turned out the lights and drew back the covers of her bed. With a bit of luck, she might get half an hour of sleep before Daisy began to whimper.

Her right foot, reaching out under the bedclothes, touched something rough and prickly. She jerked it away ... and it touched something cold and wet. She yelped and drew back her leg. Something was in her bed! What was it? She leaped out of bed and threw back the covers. It was too dark to see anything. Tentatively, she reached out her hand and slowly swept it over the mattress towards the foot of the bed.

'Arrgh!' There it was again. A round prickly shape. A suspicion was beginning to form in her mind. She felt on the top of the bedside cupboard for the box of lucifers she kept there. Her hand was shaking as she turned on the gas. The jet flared and she returned to peer apprehensively at what had been concealed in her bed.

'Arrgh!'

Lying on the sheet was a hedgehog. It was curled up, deep in its hibernating sleep. It wasn't that that nauseated her; it was the nearby saucer of worms, tipped over by her searching hand. Its contents were wriggling and writhing across the sheet.

Revolted by what she saw, she screamed. She couldn't help it. Worms were abhorrent to her. They *had* been ever since a boy had thrust a handful of them down the neck of her frock when she was six years old. Feeling the same sense of shock and revulsion, she screamed again and backed away from her bed, whimpering, 'Oh, no! No! What can I do?'

Her bedroom door crashed open.

'Miss Rossall! Whatever is the matter?'

It was Mr Dearden, still dressed in his evening attire. He strode across the room. 'Is it Daisy? Has something happened to her?'

Bea turned to him, her legs weak from the shock. Daisy was indeed crying but Bea's legs wouldn't move to go to her. 'No, no. Not Daisy. It's ...' Her voice broke and her throat closed tight. She tried to speak but words wouldn't come. She was trembling and near to tears. She pointed towards her bed....

Henry strode across the room and saw the wriggling mass of worms. He turned towards her. 'Miss Rossall. What can I say?' As he spoke, she swayed slightly and, fearing she might fall, he moved swiftly to her side and drew her into his arms.

For a moment she sank against him. He was taken aback by the surge of emotion he felt at her distress, and he longed to comfort her. Distressed and in her night attire, she seemed younger and more fragile than her usual competent air of

authority conveyed. He realized for the first time how vulnerable her position was. How easy it would be for an unprincipled
employer to take advantage of her dependence. There would be
little recourse to justice.

As though she shared his thoughts, her body tensed and she
pulled away, though he still gripped her arms just above her
elbows, keeping her steady. He guided her towards the fireside
chair. She sank on to it, her face in her hands, now sobbing
quietly.

'Sit there whilst I deal with this,' he bade her, his voice more
brusque than he intended. This was Winifred's doing, he knew
without doubt. How dare she violate her governess's bed! He
felt furious with her but stifled his anger for the time being.
His concern just now was Miss Rossall and the need to quell
the lusty demands of the baby.

'I'll bring Daisy to you,' he offered. Holding Daisy would
occupy her mind as well as her hands. 'Is it her feeding time?
Is her bottle ready?'

He had no doubt it would be and, as Bea gestured with her
hand towards the fireplace, he needed no instruction. He
picked Daisy out of her cradle, realizing it was the first time he
had held her. He felt a surge of tenderness, even though the
baby's cries were now furiously demanding that her hunger
should be satisfied. He placed her into Bea's outstretched
hands and watched with fascination as she held the baby
against her shoulder, her hand gently patting Daisy's back as
she jogged her up and down until her cries lost some of their
fury.

'Will you hand me her bottle of milk, please?'

'Oh, yes. Of course.'

He crossed over to the fire where she had gestured and
brought the bottle to her, again fascinated as she tested a drop

of milk on the back of her hand before popping the teat into Daisy's waiting mouth, bringing instant sounds of guzzling contentment. The sight tugged at his emotions. He had never thought about ever having a child of his own; he'd never met anyone with whom he wished to spend the rest of his life – but he was aware of certain stirrings deep within.

Neither of them noticed the outraged figure of Mrs Kellett framed in the open doorway until she exclaimed, 'Well! I never expected such goings on in *this* house!'

Their heads whipped round in shock.

Henry knew what his indignant housekeeper was insinuating but he was damned if he was going to give her the satisfaction of forcing him to make hurried excuses, when his presence here was totally innocent of any wrongdoing.

'"Goings on", Mrs Kellett?' He didn't miss the triumphant gleam in Mrs Kellett's eyes. 'You are referring, of course, to my nieces' misplaced sense of mischief.'

'I don't know about your nieces, Mr Dearden, but I know mischief when I see it! I warned you about 'er! Enticin' you to 'er room, no doubt! Well, she can't stay 'ere after this!'

Henry felt distinctly annoyed with Mrs Kellett. Miss Rossall was looking extremely upset and his housekeeper was relishing every moment. 'You are quite right, Mrs Kellett. She *can't* stay here.'

He heard Miss Rossall's gasp of dismay and gestured reassuringly towards her with his hand, whilst continuing to speak to his housekeeper. 'How opportune that you heard the disturbance! Whilst I am disposing of the hedgehog from Miss Rossall's bed, will you be so kind as to prepare a bed in one of the guest rooms for Miss Rossall's use.'

'A guest room?' Mrs Kellett echoed, incensed by the very idea. 'You can't—'

'Mrs Kellett, I have every confidence in your housekeeping skills,' he interrupted her before she went too far. 'I know that you regularly air each of the guest rooms, so you needn't fear that there is any danger of putting Miss Rossall into an unaired room. You may take some of the coals from the fire in my bedroom to start the fire in the guest room – and I think a drink of hot milk for Miss Rossall might help her to settle from the shock she has sustained. Thank you, Mrs Kellett. I am so thankful that you were still awake and alert.'

He felt an unaccustomed pleasure at rendering Mrs Kellett speechless and turned back towards Miss Rossall, sensing her shock at the way things were going.

'Carry on feeding Daisy, Miss Rossall,' he instructed her calmly, as if there was nothing of consequence in his decision. 'I'll return when I have disposed of these ... these creatures ... so that I can carry Daisy's cradle to your new room.'

With no more ado he set about gathering the still-sleeping hedgehog and the slippery worms into the folds of the sheet and took them downstairs. He placed the hedgehog in the woodshed, where he presumed Winifred had found it, and then shook the worms on to the garden soil.

He sighed in exasperation. What *was* he to do with Winifred? She would have to be punished, of course – and that would cause yet more resentment within her. It was one step forward and another one back with her! No wonder all previous governesses had handed in their resignations after a few weeks. At least Miss Rossall wouldn't feel able to do that! The thought pleased him. As did her agreement to being transferred to a guest room ... though it seemed to have been with a mixture of relief and bewilderment.

He bade her goodnight, promising to deal with Winifred the following morning. It was only when he lay sleepless in his own bed, reflecting on the unexpected dramatic ending to his evening, that it occurred to him that Miss Rossall had looked extremely attractive with her hair tumbling around her shoulders and her face uncluttered by her spectacles. His dreams, when at last he fell asleep, were disturbing to say the least.

Bea also spent a disturbed night and awoke feeling barely refreshed. Memories of the incident in the night did nothing to ease her. If only it weren't Sunday! She might then have been able to avoid being in Mr Dearden's presence until later in the day. Her spirit flagged. What did he think of her! And Mrs Kellett's unfortunate witnessing of the scene wouldn't improve the situation.

Would Winifred's prank bring about her dismissal? She knew Mrs Kellett would press for it ... and Mr Dearden had only promised her a month's trial. Would he see the incident as a sign of her lack of control over Winifred? Disconsolately, she picked up the bottle of warmed milk that Gertie had brought to her and began to feed Daisy. She knew she must confront Winifred as soon as possible, even if it put the girl out of humour for going to church.

When Daisy was settled she washed and dressed herself, her cheeks burning at every recollection of being held in Mr Dearden's arms attired only in her nightgown. She was furious with herself for having shown such weakness at Winifred's prank. Would he now think her to be of loose morals? She shuddered to think what would have happened if she had been put in a similar position with Cyril Ackroyd. He wouldn't have hesitated to take advantage of her predicament.

She glowered at her image in the looking-glass. Had she imagined the tenderness in Mr Dearden's eyes? In case she hadn't, she pulled her hair back into as tight a bun as she could manage and jammed her spectacles on to the bridge of her nose. There!

She stared defiantly at the austerity of her reflection. That should dampen any feelings of desire Mr Dearden might have been experiencing a few hours earlier!

Later, her breakfast over, she went to the day nursery and requested that the girls accompany her to the schoolroom. Winifred presented a challenging glint in her eyes. She made no attempt to deny her guilt.

'It was a joke,' she said carelessly.

'A poor sort of joke, Winifred. I don't suppose the hedgehog found it funny.'

'It was asleep. I thought it would be happier somewhere warmer than the woodshed.'

'So you chose my bed. Why not your own, since you were the one so anxious about its welfare?'

Winifred shrugged, a glimmer of a smile twitching her lips. 'It wouldn't have been so funny.'

'No, I don't suppose it would. I am disappointed in you, Winifred.'

Winifred flushed and looked slightly ashamed. It didn't last. She flung back her hair again and looked defiant. 'So, I suppose you're going to punish me. I don't care.'

'Maybe you don't – but you *should* care, because any punishment inflicted on you is likely to affect Lily, too, so it's a bit selfish of you, isn't it?'

Winifred hung her head, her right foot drawing small circles on the floor. 'It doesn't have to affect Lily. I s'pose you'll stop me doing something I like.'

'Yes. I'm afraid wrongdoing always has some sort of consequence. In this case you will spend this afternoon looking through a book on wildlife that I spotted in your uncle's library, and write a short composition on hedgehogs and their natural habitat. I have planned to take Daisy out in her pram this afternoon, since it is such a nice day, so I will leave you with Nanny Adams whilst Lily comes with me and Daisy.'

After a flash of resentment in her eyes, Winifred obviously decided she was being let off comparatively lightly. 'I don't care! I don't want to go out with Daisy.'

'I also think an apology is in order,' Bea continued.

'But I'm not sorry.'

'Then you must search your heart to find an aspect of the incident that you *can* be sorry about,' Bea pronounced. 'In the meantime, you need to be getting ready for church. Don't keep your uncle waiting again, as you did last week.'

It was a silent, subdued group that made its way down the hill to Holy Trinity church. The Hawsleys were already in their pew and Miss Hawsley made a point of bestowing a ladylike inclination of her head in Mr Dearden's direction as he stood aside to allow Bea and the girls to enter the pew before him. He reciprocated with a polite bow.

After the service, Miss Hawsley left her pew at the same time as the Deardens and she straight away claimed Mr Dearden's arm.

'Dinner at Ridgmont House last evening was so delightful, wasn't it?' she gushed. 'We have already let the Howarths know of our pleasure and begged their presence at a similar occasion at our home in the not-too-distant future. I hope we can also count upon you, Mr Dearden. People of our standing make agreeable company at such social occasions, do you not agree?'

'It was certainly a very agreeable gathering last evening,' Bea heard him reply, as she followed them down the aisle towards the porch. 'I shall look forward to receiving your invitation.'

'Excellent! Mama was saying only this morning how well we do together.' Miss Hawsley glanced coyly at him, obviously awaiting a response.

Winifred was exchanging 'sick-looking' faces with Lily, compelling Bea to twitch their arms in order to remind them that such actions were inappropriate, especially as they were now standing in line to bid the vicar good morning.

Bea couldn't help wondering at the friendship between her employer and the haughty Miss Hawsley. They seemed so ill-matched. Her manner, and that of her parents, bordered on arrogance. Was Mr Dearden attracted to them? Did he aspire to be counted among the social elite, as they so obviously did?

She was annoyed to find that the thought disturbed her.

Chapter 11

CAROLINE HAWSLEY FELT distinctly annoyed. She had expected Henry Dearden to be eating out of her hand by now. Everything had seemed to be falling her way. He had accompanied her to a number of engagements and had had dinner with them several times. Why was he holding back?

Maybe she should have made her move earlier, before those troublesome nieces had come to live with him – though why his feckless brother had chosen to go off to America in so much of a hurry, she didn't know. And why hadn't he returned as soon as his wife had died? But for his daughters, she might have made a play for *him* – he was far more outgoing than his elder brother. But, maybe not, his life style was hardly likely to endear him to the local society, and that was an important factor in her choice of a husband.

No, she had made the better choice, but he wasn't as easily influenced as she had expected. Of course, he was more reserved than his brother and, as far as she knew, had never shown more than a casual interest in any young lady. Local gossip indicated that he intended to make his way in his chosen field of engineering before settling down with a wife and children, which was why she hadn't been in any hurry to set out to attract him to her side.

Now, however, he seemed to be taking his role as the girls'

temporary guardian more seriously than she had at first thought. Surely something hadn't happened to his brother, so that he knew that his role was to last for longer than he had supposed? No, he would have said something. Wouldn't he?

She paced about her bedroom. What could she do to attract his attention? Maybe she should try to gain favour with his nieces. She shuddered slightly. The elder one in particular was a troublesome girl. Still, it need only be for a short time. If their feckless father did not return to claim them soon, the first thing she would do upon becoming the new Mrs Dearden would be to pack them off to a boarding school – preferably one in North Yorkshire or, better still, Northumberland.

What a pity the previous governess had left so abruptly – and with Miss Rossall ready to hand on the doorstep. Miss Pilling would have been a better replacement. She would have soon brought a firm line of discipline into their lives. Perhaps it might be possible to expose Miss Rossall as being incompetent? After all, a vicar's daughter from the inner-city slums could hardly know much about educating young ladies of *their* class. Once more without a governess, Henry would be sure to engage Miss Pilling and his nieces would be as good as gone already!

After continual rain on Monday morning, the girls were fractious with each other. After lunch, Bea told the girls the story of the runaway gingerbread man.

'And now, we will make our very own gingerbread men,' she announced with a smile. 'Let's go and ask Mrs Kellett when will be the best time to make them.'

'No time's the best time!' Mrs Kellett replied tartly. 'I can't be 'avin' no children messin' about in my kitchen!'

'Oh!' Bea was confused for a moment. 'Well, we *could* do all the mixing and shaping in the schoolroom,' she amended her plan, 'but I will need to bring the tray down here to bake them.'

With bad grace, Mrs Kellett banged down packets of the various ingredients Bea required on to the kitchen table. With a calmness she didn't feel, Bea placed the items on a tray and moved the girls back to the schoolroom where they tackled the new experience of making something they could eat with enthusiasm. Chatting and laughing together as they rolled the shapes to make the gingerbread men, Bea felt that more barriers were being broken down. When all of the mixture had been shaped and placed on to two baking-trays, they carried them carefully down to the kitchen.

Gertie, almost smothered by a voluminous apron, was seated at a corner of the table cleaning some silver. She looked up at the children. Her face split into a wide grin. 'Yer've got flour on yer faces!'

Lily giggled and wiped the back of her hand across her face, smudging yet more flour there – but Winifred scowled at Gertie.

'Take a look at yourself. Your face is dirty! Dirty Gertie!' she taunted. 'Don't get shirty, dirty Gertie!'

Sure enough, Gertie had streaks of the grey paste smudged across her face. Her face reddened at Winifred's taunts and, with an uncomfortable glance at Mrs Kellett, she muttered, 'I'm sorry, miss. I didn't mean nothin'.' She hung her head and rubbed more furiously at the spoon in her hand.

'Winifred, that's not kind,' Bea reprimanded. 'Tell Gertie you are sorry for calling her names.'

'I shan't!' Winnie refused 'She started it! And she is dirty! She shouldn't be at the table looking like that!'

'Gertie is working, Winifred. And she didn't call you names;

she merely made an observation. So, apologize quickly and we will say no more.'

Winifred's face set in a mutinous scowl. 'Shan't!'

'Very well, Winifred. Put down your tray and return to the schoolroom. I will speak to you later.'

Winifred glared defiantly at her but, when Bea calmly held her gaze, she banged the baking-tray down on to the table and ran from the kitchen. Bea let out her breath. Another problem to sort out!

She smiled at Gertie. 'You are doing a fine job there, Gertie. It's one I have done many a time, myself – and isn't it satisfying when the silver is nice and shiny again? I think one of these gingerbread men will make a nice reward for you. Now, Lily, put down your tray and I will show you the oven where Mrs Kellett will bake our gingerbread men. Don't touch it, because it will be very hot.'

She spent a few minutes talking about how Mrs Kellett would make sure the oven was at the correct heat before putting the baking-trays into it and that she would look at the clock to see what time it was and would remove the trays when the gingerbread men were baked. 'So, let's return to the schoolroom and draw a picture of a gingerbread man and write a few words about how you made him.'

As she opened the door that led back into the main part of the house, a high-pitched scream sounded from upstairs. Even as Bea started forward in alarm, she knew it wasn't Winifred or Nanny Adams who had screamed. So, who was it?

As more screaming and a furious tirade of abuse jagged its way down the stairs, the door of Mr Dearden's study was flung open and Mr Dearden stormed out. 'What on earth is going on, Miss Rossall? Who...?' A dawning of understanding flowed over his face and he hurried towards the stairs. He reached the foot of the staircase at the same time as Bea. Their eyes were drawn upwards by the approaching sounds from above. Winifred's screams and protests were now mingled with the older tones.

Bea and Henry glanced at each other in a mixture of alarm and consternation and both started to ascend the staircase together. They only got as far as putting one foot each on the lowest stair when two figures whirled into view on the mid-landing. Miss Hawsley, covered in flour from head to foot, was dragging Winifred along by her scrunched-up hair. Winifred was not coming quietly.

'Let me go! You're hurting me! I've told you! It wasn't meant for you!'

'I don't care who it was meant for, you wretched child! You need to be taught a lesson on how to behave! Just wait till your uncle hears of this! He'll soon send that useless governess packing! Oh!' Her voice broke off in surprise as she saw the two named adults at the foot of the stairs, with Mrs Kellett, Gertie and Lily a few steps behind them. A momentary falter was quickly overcome. 'Just look what this obnoxious child has done?' she said angrily. 'She set a flour trap for me! My clothes are ruined! She deserves a good whipping!' She continued to drag Winifred down the stairs as she spoke, oblivious to the danger of either one of them missing their footing and falling headlong.

Henry leaped up the remaining steps and restrained Miss Hawsley's grip on Winifred's hair. 'Miss Rossall will now see to Winifred, Miss Hawsley. Come along to my sitting room and Mrs Kellett will assist you to ... er ... do what you can to remedy the matter. Would you be so kind, Mrs Kellett?' He glanced over his shoulder. 'Take Winifred upstairs, Miss Rossall. I will be with you as soon as I am able.' He led the still volubly protesting young woman towards his sitting room, offering soothing comments.

Bea turned to Winifred. 'Upstairs, young lady,' she said grimly. She saw Nanny Adams hovering on the mid-landing. 'Lily, go to the nursery with Nanny Adams. I think it's time for our afternoon drink. Winifred, come with me to the schoolroom. You have some explaining to do.'

Winifred displayed little repentance. Instead, she glowered with rebellion and resentment. 'It isn't fair! Gertie was just as unkind to me. You didn't tell *her* to apologize, so why should *I?*'

'Gertie merely spoke without thinking,' Bea explained patiently. 'She wasn't being unkind. I expect she thought you would laugh about it, like Lily did. When she is older and has more experience, she will realize that, as a servant, she shouldn't pass comment on the appearance of members of the household. As it is, she is still a child. No doubt she will learn from this and she *did* apologize. The thing is, Winifred, we are in a privileged position over the servants. Whatever we say to them, they cannot answer back without being in danger of losing their job. This makes them very vulnerable – and some people misuse their power over them and make their life intolerable. I know that that isn't your intention. You aren't an unkind girl.'

Winifred threw her a look from under her eyelashes and quickly lowered her gaze again. Bea wasn't sure whether the look was of guilt or remorse. 'What I would like you to do, Winifred, is to give Gertie one of the gingerbread men you made when we go down to collect them and say you are sorry for calling her names. As for Miss Hawsley, I fear she will demand a more detailed apology, so start thinking about what you are going to say to her. Now, let's start clearing this flour away before it gets trodden in all over the house.'

They were still in the process of doing that when Mr Dearden made his appearance. Having been harangued for over five minutes by Miss Hawsley about Winifred's wildness and Miss Rossall's total unsuitability, he was in no mood to mince his words. 'Winifred, I have had enough of such behaviour! You will go downstairs and apologize to Miss Hawsley at once. Then you will return here to hear what punishment is to be given. Go, now!'

With a backward glance over her shoulder, Winifred left the room. Bea hoped she did exactly as Mr Dearden had bade her. She awaited his indictment on her.

'Winifred is obviously out of control! I think it is time to say enough is enough – and send her away to school somewhere!'

Bea was shocked. 'No! You can't mean it! Her world has already been turned upside down in the past few years. Her family life has all but disintegrated. She's struggling to find her new identity. It can't be easy for her.'

'It isn't easy for any of us, her sister included – but Lily doesn't seem to find it too difficult to behave herself.'

'Lily is younger – and of a different character,' Bea said quietly.

He raised an eyebrow. 'It has been mentioned, Miss Rossall, that you allow the girls far too much liberality both in their speech and their behaviour! I am sure you are familiar with the saying, "Spare the rod and spoil the child"!'

He suspected that Miss Rossall was not deterred by his sardonic query, although she *was* greatly discomfited, as was obvious from the pink flush of her cheeks and the way she agitatedly pushed her spectacles more firmly on the bridge of her nose – but she eyed him quite determinedly. Had he been foolish in treating her more like his equal than an employee – as Miss Hawsley had just warned him?

He sighed impatiently. His life used to be run on an even keel, whereas now he felt trapped between two opposite views. But which offered the counsel nearest to his own desire? Miss Hawsley's solution would bring some peace back into his life – but would it also encourage Miss Hawsley to attempt to interfere too much in his life? When she had called, expressing her wish to get to know his nieces a bit better, he had asked her to wait in his sitting room until her could accompany her upstairs to the schoolroom – a suggestion she had flagrantly ignored. Neither did he expect Miss Rossall to agree quietly to the solution offered.

'Well?' he almost barked, noting with some satisfaction that Miss Rossall flinched at his tone. Good! Maybe she wasn't as totally sure of herself as she would have him believe!

'I don't condone Winifred's behaviour,' she began hesitantly, 'and she must learn that she cannot be so disrespectful of the feelings of others – but I don't think sending her away is the best course of action. She is a very unhappy little girl.'

'We are all unhappy!' he snapped. 'I'm unhappy to have my home life disrupted! You are no doubt unhappy to have lost your father and your home. Good heavens! What would happen if we took it into our heads to disrupt everyone around us? A fine state the world would be in!'

'Yes, indeed – but we are not ten years old. We have learned to modify our behaviour. But I can remember how lost and lonely I felt when *my* mother died when I was only a year or so older than Winifred is now. I felt I would never be happy again!'

'Maybe – but I cannot believe that you reacted as Winifred does!'

'No, but don't forget, I still had my father to love and care for me.'

'Winifred still has *her* father!'

'Yes, but he's not here! He may as well be dead, too, as far as Winifred is concerned! And she has been uprooted from her home and all her friends! The only links she has with her past are Lily and Nanny Adams. Everything else has changed. Even her governesses have changed with a frequency that can only be harmful. It must surely add to her confusion!'

Good grief! Did she think he didn't know all of this? He wasn't completely unfeeling, however lowly she might regard him! 'Then what is your answer to all of this, Miss Rossall?' he asked coldly. 'I presume you have one!'

He saw her passionate spirit deflate in front of him. Her shoulders sagged and she ruefully grimaced. 'I haven't got an infallible answer,' she admitted candidly. 'I just feel we should show her more love and understanding; boost her confidence a bit; allow her time and space to come to terms with her losses – without falling upon her like a ton of bricks every time she misbehaves.'

'So, we just do nothing? Is that what you suggest?'

'No – but try not to show anger. Anger makes her feel unloved – and I am sure that is not the case.'

Oh, so she did credit him with some finer feelings! 'Very well, Miss Rossall, I will give Winifred one more chance. I hope she responds to your faith in her, though I cannot say I have much expectation of that. Be warned though – the very next time Winifred steps out of line, I shall make arrangements to send her away to a boarding school and see if a harsher regime has more effect on her behaviour.'

Winifred was much quieter over the next few days. Bea was still troubled about her. Winifred was *too* quiet. She was morose, brooding, scowling with resentment whenever Daisy was being attended to. However, she was doing well at her lessons and Bea hoped she was worrying needlessly.

The weather improved towards the end of the week and on Friday Bea decided they would walk into the small town to explore some of its many streets in the morning, then they could record their observations on the tracing she had made of a map of Horwich that Mr Dearden had loaned her from the railway works in the afternoon and over the weekend. It was a lovely spring day, so she took Daisy as well, propped up against a cushion in the perambulator, held in place by a set of reins that had been found among the bag of baby clothes.

It was almost lunchtime when they arrived home and she left the children to play in the garden while she went indoors to let Mrs Kellett know they were back home and would welcome their lunch as soon as it was convenient. When she returned to the garden, all was quiet. There was no sign of the girls. At first Bea wasn't unduly worried as neither girl had ever made any attempt to leave the garden unaccompanied. But when she went to make sure Daisy was still sleeping peacefully the pram was empty.

She felt a stab of alarm. Where was Daisy? Had the girls taken her out of the pram and were playing with her in another part of the garden?

'Winifred? Lily?' she called. 'Where are you?' She ran towards the shrubbery and heard a stifled giggle. It was Lily, crouching down among the bushes. 'Lily! There you are! Come here! Where's Winifred?'

Lily crawled out, beaming at Bea. 'She's hiding. We're playing hide-and-seek. Now I'll have to be "it" after you've found Winifred.'

Bea felt her panic subdue slightly. 'Has Winifred got Daisy with her?'

'Daisy?' Lily looked at her blankly. 'No, she's just hiding somewhere. You have to find her.'

'Then where's Daisy?' She knew she had spoken sharply, but she couldn't help it.

Lily looked perplexed. 'Isn't she in the pram?'

'No.' Bea looked around frantically. 'Winifred! Come out from wherever you are!'

She began to run round the garden, her anxiety growing with every passing second. She caught sight of Winifred hiding behind a tree and ran through the shrubbery towards her, heedless of the low branches that caught at her, scratching her face and hands as she thrust them aside.

Knowing she was discovered, Winifred stepped into view. Bea pulled up sharply. Winifred was alone. 'Where's Daisy, Winifred?' she demanded.

Winifred laughed wildly. 'You'll have to catch me!' she called, whirling away out of the shrubbery and into the small orchard.

Bea set off after her, her heart pounding. What had Winifred done with Daisy?

Chapter 12

BEA FELT A stitch in her side. She held on to the trunk of a tree, gasping for breath. Where was Daisy? Her legs suddenly lost their strength and she sank down on to the grass. Sobs erupted from her throat and tears ran down her cheeks.

Aware that she wasn't alone, she looked up and saw Winifred standing a couple of feet away, watching her, her face portraying some inner emotion that Bea couldn't guess at. She gestured towards her with her hand. 'I'm sorry, Winifred. Of course you've not hidden her.' She struggled to her feet. 'Let's get help to find her.'

Winifred stood her ground. 'You love her more than you love us!' she accused. 'She's only a baby. We'd be better without her. Mama said so.'

Bea paused. 'What are you saying?'

Winifred hung her head for a moment. When she looked up, tears welled in her eyes. 'Mama said she didn't want another baby. She said she couldn't bear to have it. It was too much to ask of her.' Her voice was flat but held a note of authenticity.

Bea was puzzled. No mention had been made of their mama having another baby. Had she miscarried it? Or worse, had she died in childbirth and the baby died too? Was that why Winifred was so antagonistic towards Daisy?

She put her hand on Winifred's shoulder. 'Babies need a lot of care, and sometimes the thought of having another baby can seem to be a great burden, especially if the mama is unwell – but she would love the baby when it came. She wouldn't have wanted anyone to take it away.'

'She must have. We never got another baby and then mama died and they put her in the cold dark ground. She would still be here but for that baby.'

Bea drew Winifred towards her and bent down so that her face was level with Winifred's. 'I'm sorry your mama died, Winifred. I know how you feel. My mama died when I was just a bit older than you. I missed her a lot. I still do, at times. But Daisy isn't the baby your mama was talking about. Daisy's mama asked me to look after Daisy for her. That's why she is here with me.'

Bea suddenly felt sure Winifred knew where Daisy was. 'Why don't you show me and Lily where Daisy is and then we can go in and see what Mrs Kellett is making for our lunch?' She held out both hands to the girls. 'Come on, let's go and get her, shall we?'

Lily took hold of the hand nearest to her and, after a slight pause, Winifred took hold of the other. 'I wasn't going to leave her there,' she said quietly. 'It's just ... she always has you or Nanny Adams looking after her. You always go to her whenever she cries.'

'That's because babies are so dependent on whoever is looking after them. She'll never know her own mama but we can all help her not to miss her mama too much, can't we?'

'Has her papa gone away, like ours has?' Lily asked. 'She could share our papa when he comes back, couldn't she? When he comes home, that is.'

'I don't think he's coming home,' Winifred said sadly. She

was guiding them out of the shrubbery and across the lawn towards the vegetable garden. Bea could guess now where they were heading but she stood still as Winifred continued: 'Mama told him to go away and never come back. That's why she died. She said he had broken her heart.'

Bea put her arms round both girls and drew them to her. 'Sometimes, when people are upset, they say things they don't really mean. Your papa would have realized that she was upset about something and didn't really mean it. I know your mama loved you both very much and your papa still does. He'll come as soon as he can. I'm sure he will.'

Bea offered a fervent silent prayer that her words would come true. Whatever his differences with his wife, surely he would come to claim his children when he learned of his wife's death? After another hug, she straightened up again. 'Come on. Let's get Daisy, shall we?'

She let Winifred lead them towards the garden shed. As they drew near, they could hear the sounds of Daisy crying and it took all of Bea's self-control not to let go of the children's hands and run the remaining distance.

'I can hear her!' Lily cried. She ran forward and opened the door. 'What a good hiding place, Winifred! It was better than mine!'

Bea decided it was best to leave Lily with that notion, though she added, 'But we'll not let Daisy play hide-and-seek again until she's a bit older, eh girls?'

She was troubled by aspects of what Winifred had said and, that evening during dinner, without saying anything about Winifred having hidden Daisy, she told Mr Dearden what Winifred had said regarding another baby.

Mr Dearden pondered her words but shook his head. 'I know nothing of another baby, though it's true that my sister-in-law was very troubled during the last few months of her life. Winifred must have misheard an adult conversation. However, if that is what has been causing Winifred's bad behaviour, let us hope that, now it has been brought to light, her behaviour will show a great improvement.'

Bea understood his hopes but could not really share his optimism.

Winifred was quite subdued throughout the rest of the day. It was during Daisy's bath time that Bea discovered what was still troubling her. As Bea undressed Daisy, she could see the tiny bruises still present on her arms and legs. Winifred went quiet. She was kneeling on the carpet near the bathtub and she sank back on to her heels and hung her head.

'It's me who's been pinching her,' she muttered quietly. 'It didn't seem fair when she got all the attention, just because she's a baby. I'm sorry. I won't do it again, I promise.' She raised her eyes and looked sorrowfully at Bea. 'And I thought, if I was really naughty Uncle Henry would make Papa come back and take us back home.'

Bea leaned towards her and hugged her. 'Oh, Winifred, your uncle is doing all he can to find out where your papa is – not because he doesn't want you here but because he knows how much you miss your papa. Now, look, Daisy is smiling at you.'

And she was. Daisy opportunely gurgled and waved her chubby arms and legs in the air in gleeful ecstasy at being freed from her restrictive clothing. For the first time, Winifred looked delighted at a response from Daisy.

Winifred's confession seemed to lessen her desire to rebel. She became more attentive in the classroom and her drawing improved also.

One evening at dinner Bea showed Mr Dearden Winifred's

detailed drawing of the town hall. 'She has a good eye for detail and perspective. We must encourage her in that direction; maybe even to let her see your designs on the drawing board?'

'To what purpose, Miss Rossall? There are no ladies working in the locomotive works drawing office; nor in any other drawing office that I know of.'

Bea smiled. 'Maybe not today, nor even next year, but we are approaching the start of a new century, Mr Dearden, and who is to say what changes we shall see during it?'

Henry smiled. 'You really think that by the time Winifred is of an age to enter into the working world, she will be able to take a place from a young man who is already being groomed for such a position?'

'Of course. All she needs is the right training and the right opportunities!'

'And the right employer who will see things as you do, Miss Rossall. At the moment, any prospective employer would see too many hindrances in such an idea!'

'Such as getting married, I suppose? Education is never wasted. Which parent do you suppose has a greater influence on their children in their younger years? It is their mother, Mr Dearden! Mothers are the ones who guide future generations – and just think what better guidance an *educated* woman will be able to give her children!'

Henry looked sceptical. 'I am almost persuaded, Miss Rossall. However, in this instance, it is not I whom you need to persuade but my brother. And I doubt you will find much agreement from him on such matters. He had little enough interest in his own education.'

'Then you must do all you can to make him see things differently. Do you know how long he is likely to be away?'

'No, Miss Rossall, I do not. My brother, unfortunately, tends to think only of himself. In the meantime, however, I see no reason why you should not give a good grounding to my nieces' education. I only hope it does not make them dissatisfied with their limited opportunities when their education is complete.'

'And I hope it *will* make them dissatisfied, Mr Dearden, for it is only out of dissatisfaction with the present that the future will be changed.'

Winifred showed great interest in her uncle's work on his drawing board and, after he had seen more of Winifred's drawings, he brought home some large pieces of drawing paper, and also a drawing board, solely for her use. She found the task of drawing absorbing and Henry was pleasurably surprised by the improved standard of her work.

He found himself extolling his niece's skill at the Hawsleys' dinner party the following week and dealt swiftly with Miss Hawsleys' disparaging remarks about Winifred's behaviour, adding that it was Miss Rossall's expertise that had brought about the improvement.

'In my opinion, Miss Rossall has very strange ideas about what is suitable education for the daughters of gentlemen!' Mrs Hawsley said sharply. 'I would not want a daughter of mine to set her mind on such things! Young girls of our class should be reared genteelly. Their highest aim should be that of becoming a good wife and a graceful hostess.'

When some of the other guests murmured their agreement, Henry expressed the wish that they could have the opportunity to hear Miss Rossall's views first-hand.

A week later, on a windy day at the bginning of April, Henry was making his way home when he remembered his nieces' plea for a kite. So over the next couple of days, he gathered together the necessary materials, delighting in recapturing his youthful skill in making a kite.

It was the week before Easter and he found himself planning an outing for his household. He would ask Miss Rossall not to arrange any activities for Good Friday afternoon.

'All I will say is that the treat is to take place after the morning service at church – and you must all wear outdoor clothing and sturdy boots,' he said enigmatically, after making the invitation.

'All?' Bea queried, her heart leaping with anticipation. 'I am included? And Daisy?'

'Of course. Besides, I am not yet that confident with my nieces that I can anticipate their needs or reactions without your stabilizing presence. No, you may take your presence as an obligatory requirement for my peace of mind.' *And* his enjoyment, he realized, as the momentary thought of the outing without her filled him with dismay.

Consequently, as they returned from church on Good Friday morning, Winifred, Lily and Bea were excited to see two hired dog-carts waiting outside Endmoor House. Daisy's cradle was already loaded in the second cart, balanced on top of a wickerwork picnic basket. Nanny Adams had already wrapped up Daisy in a warm shawl, although she herself had opted to remain at home. Gertie was jumping up and down in excitement. Mrs Kellett and Gregson were standing by, with only Mrs Kellett showing any antipathy towards the planned outing.

Streams of people were making their way up Chorley Old Road and when the two dog-carts turned into George's Lane, Bea knew their destination. She realized it must be a local tradition for the local people of Horwich to make the pilgrimage up Rivington Pike on this holy day.

The dog-carts halted on a level part of the track just below the summit of the hill. 'Out you all get,' Mr Dearden announced. 'Gregson and Mrs Kellett are going to remain here to unload the picnic whilst the rest of us scramble up to the top. Yes, and you, too, Gertie; this is your treat as well. Put Daisy in her cradle, Miss Rossall. Mrs Kellett will keep a good eye on her.'

Bea glanced down at Daisy. The baby's eyes were already closing, so she did as Mr Dearden suggested. Oh, it was good to scramble with others up the roughly grassed uneven slope of the pike. The girls scampered ahead, with Gertie trying to keep pace with them. At last they stood triumphant, jostling for space with other children on the stone base of the watchtower.

As Henry watched the children scampering around the tower he realized that he was enjoying himself. It crossed his mind that this could have been his own family, if he had met and married someone with whom he felt he wanted to spend the rest of his life – only he never had. He had left all of that to his younger brother, who didn't seem to appreciate what he had got.

A picture of Miss Rossall holding Daisy in her arms in the dog-cart presented itself in his mind, followed by a previous, more intimate memory of her feeding the baby on the night of Winifred's prank with the hedgehog. A lurch of his heart took him by surprise. Was it yet possible that he might have the joy of seeing a child of his own thus held? Still musing on that startling thought, Henry led the way back to where the picnic had been set out and they tucked into the sandwiches, pastries and cakes that Mrs Kellett had prepared.

'And this is not all,' Henry said, when most of the food had been eaten. He stood up, brushing some crumbs off his trousers. 'Wait there while I get the next part.'

He ran lightly down to the dog-carts and rummaged in the back of the one the servants had travelled in. When he came back he had something tucked under his arm He placed it on the ground and began to put it together.

'It's a kite!' the girls squealed in delight. 'Oh, Uncle Henry, you remembered!'

'I did indeed. Now, let's just fit these strips of wood in the right places and make sure the string is securely attached. There! Come on. Let's put it to the test.'

The wind was stronger at the top of the hill than down the slope and the kite soared easily into the sky. Henry pulled at the string a few times to get it as high as he could and then handed the bobbin of string to Winifred. 'Like this,' he bade her, pulling on the string once more.

Lily and Gertie had their turns and Henry and Bea stood in companionable contentment watching the three girls having fun. It was a very happy party who returned home.

As they were clambering out of the dog-carts a fine carriage was being driven past and a female voice hailed gaily, 'Good afternoon, Mr Dearden! Stop, Hogg!'

At the imperious tones, Bea's heart sank. It was Miss Hawsley and another lady. Miss Hawsley had been very cool towards the girls since the incident with the flour. Was she about to spoil what had been a lovely day?

Henry raised his hat. 'Good afternoon, Miss Hawsley. Miss Ingham. How good to see you. When you weren't in church this morning, I feared you were unwell. Have you enjoyed your drive?'

'Indeed we have,' Miss Hawsley replied, twirling her small parasol over her head. 'We have been visiting Wallsuches House. A pity you weren't one of the party, Mr Dearden, though I believe you were invited.' Her glance quickly scanned the rest of Mr Dearden's group, now making their way through the garden gate. 'I see you have been entertaining your nieces. Very noble of you, although I am sure they might have been included in the invitation if you had asked.'

Her gaze fastened on to the sight of the governess with a baby in her arms. Her eyebrows rose to their limit. 'I didn't know that there was a baby in your household, Mr Dearden? To whom does it belong? It cannot be part of your brother's family, or its presence would have been known before now.'

Henry bristled at the impertinence of her comment. 'You are quite right, Miss Hawsley. Daisy is a recent addition to our household but Nanny Adams is quite capable of taking care of her.'

He deliberately made no mention of Miss Rossall, suspecting that Miss Hawsley would make as much as she could of such a connection. Though, judging by Miss Hawsley's raised eyebrow and the curl of her lip as she watched Miss Rossall usher the girls into the house ahead of her, with the baby held against her with practised ease, he suspected that she had made the connection anyway.

'Really? Well, well,' she mused, pursed her lips.

Henry felt angered by the insinuations she was making but bit back a caustic reply. With Miss Ingham present he had no wish to provoke an unpleasant scene. He masked his feelings and remained silent.

Miss Hawsley looked at him quizzically, as if awaiting a response. When none was forthcoming, her lips parted in a smile, rather like that of a crocodile, he couldn't help thinking. 'Well, we must bid you good day, Mr Dearden. Oh, I presume you will be attending the performance of Handel's *Messiah* at the Mechanics' Institute tomorrow evening? Good. I look forward to seeing you there. Drive on, Hogg.'

Henry was relieved to see her carriage depart. He couldn't understand the strange emotion surging within him. After all, he knew that Miss Hawsley had a fine sense of her own family's importance, as had both her parents. There was nothing new in that. No, what was new was his reaction to it. He found himself to be highly indignant that she should look down her nose at her social inferiors in general and at Miss Rossall in particular. Miss Rossall was the daughter of a vicar, for goodness' sake! Miss Hawsley didn't act in such a manner towards the Reverend Pigot. Why, he and Mrs Pigot had been guests at the Hawsleys' dining table only last week.

He tried to imagine Miss Hawsley scrambling up Rivington Pike with his nieces or flying a kite on a windy day – but he knew it was impossible. To be fair, he wouldn't have pictured himself doing those things only a few weeks ago. Then, the constant sense of disruption to his well-ordered life had irritated him beyond belief; as had the numerous complaints made by the string of governesses about his nieces' behaviour. Not once had he felt inclined to join in any of their activities.

He knew he felt differently now. He also knew that it was due to Miss Rossall; a prim-looking yet fun-loving spinster daughter of a city vicar, who, with little experience of upper-middle class society, knew how to treat people with respect and dignity, even a lowly kitchen maid and his cantankerous housekeeper.

She was a governess in a million, he thought benignly. He sincerely hoped she would stay until his nieces had left his care.

Now, that was a sobering thought. How empty the house would then be!

Chapter 13

MORE EXCITEMENT FOLLOWED on the Saturday, when the young men of Horwich raced each other from the gates of the railway works, through the town to the top of Rivington Pike, cheered on their way by many onlookers, happy to be free from their daily work.

Winifred daringly joined some boys who were running along the pavements, trying to keep up with the runners. Her eyes flashed with rebellion when Bea called her back.

'Boys have a much better time than girls,' she complained.

'So they do,' Bea agreed with her, causing the light in Winifred's eyes to change from rebellion to interest. 'But I think that all that will change in the future.'

'Really? How?'

'By us females showing that we are just as capable as they are. Not many are ready to listen yet – but our time will come. We must make sure we are ready. Seize the opportunities that come your way, Winifred.'

Winifred nodded. She liked the sound of that. Maybe their governess wasn't so bad, after all.

The success of the Easter outings made Henry consider other aspects of his previously austere life style that might be changed. He was a popular guest at various dinner tables among the upper reaches of society in Horwich. Maybe it was time to reciprocate in kind – but whom could he ask to act as his hostess? He suspected Mrs Hawsley would leap at the chance, should he offer it – but that would create speculation as to his intentions.

He frowned. Had he already unwittingly placed Miss Hawsley in an insidious position? Had she been reading too much into the frequency of their social engagements? He hoped not – though he often detected a proprietorial air in Miss Hawsley's manner towards him. In the past, it had amused him, lately it had begun to irritate him.

So, how was he to follow his inclination to hold a dinner party in his home? He sat upright: he had the very answer! He would flout convention and dispense with the role of a hostess altogether.

Consequently, just over a week later, he took delight in telling Miss Rossall that he had decided to host a dinner party at his home on Saturday 30 April. 'I have invited a number of guests, ten in all, which will make us twelve at table: an ideal number for this first dinner party, don't you think?'

Bea was listening with polite interest, her mind being more preoccupied with the discrepancy in Mr Dearden's mathematics – insofar as ten guests plus himself made eleven diners, not twelve – than in the exact implication of his words.

With no comment yet forthcoming from her, Henry regarded her quizzically. 'What, no comment, Miss Rossall? I expected a glimmer of excitement at the very least. Maybe even a murmur of doubt, though I would hastily brush that aside. You do at least think it is a good idea, do you not? I felt that it is high time that I should reciprocate the many pleasant evenings I have enjoyed in the houses of my many friends and associates.'

Bea laughed at his boyish excitement. 'It is an excellent plan, Mr Dearden and I am sure your friends will feel highly honoured to be at your very first dinner party. Do you need *my* help in any way? To wait at table, perhaps or to help with any of the preparations, the table decorations?'

Henry stared at her aghast. 'Wait at table? Indeed not!'

Bea felt a momentary pang, hurt that he should think her inadequate for that menial task – but the hurt had barely registered when he continued to speak.

'You are to be a guest, Miss Rossall.'

Bea stared at him open-mouthed. She must have misheard him.

'What did you say?' She knew she was gaping like a goldfish and swallowed hard, taking great effort to close her mouth. 'A guest? But I can't be. I won't.'

Henry smiled. 'And why not, Miss Rossall? Do you consider yourself to be superior to my other guests?'

Bea glared at him. 'You know very well that that is not so,' she snapped.

'Ah, then, you consider my other guests to be superior to you? But, how can that be, since you don't yet know who they are?'

'No, I do not consider your other guests to be superior to me. I just suspect that they might *think* they are!'

'Ah. Then let us see. Reverend and Mrs Pigot?'

Bea narrowed her eyes. 'You are playing with me. You know very well Reverend and Mrs Pigot will not look down upon me.'

'Good. That's two who pass muster. Mr Horace Cooke, the owner of a local paper mill, and his wife?'

'I don't know them,' Bea admitted shortly.

'I am happy to say, they are both very congenial. As are Mr Daniel Brownlow and his wife. Mr Brownlow, as well as being a local businessman, is one of the bellringers at Holy Trinity; rather a tradition in his family I believe. You see, I am making it easy for you.'

'Maybe. That is only six guests. You said ten, did you not?'

'I did. Doctor Jacobs is the seventh guest. You haven't met him yet, either, but he is a very estimable young man. An ophthalmic optician is what he calls himself. I am sure you will like him. I must admit I have invited him especially so that you might meet him.'

'Oh?'

'Yes. I feel a little concerned that your eyes may need further correction. You sometimes seem a little ... er ... distracted at times, as if things are not in focus. No, no, don't take offence. I mean it kindly.'

Bea knew her cheeks had flushed with guilt. His words were so true. Her eyes were frequently out of focus, since her papa's spectacles had been made to correct *his* vision, not *hers* – but how was she to admit it? 'That might be helpful,' she admitted, slowly. Her spirits were rising. She felt she could cope with the guests named so far. 'That leaves three more guests,' she reminded him.

'Ah, yes. Now, these are the three with whom you may feel a little uncomfortable.' He hesitated and Bea began to suspect who they might be. Her fears were confirmed when he continued: 'The Hawsleys. Yes, I know they think themselves superior to anyone who has to work for their living – but that includes everyone else who will be at the table, myself included. I cannot pass them over. I have eaten at their table more than anywhere else. They would have the right to be offended if they were not invited to my first dinner party.'

Bea felt dismayed. Her presence at the dinner table would be a surprise to all of the guests, although the first seven mentioned would have the good manners to pretend otherwise – but not the Hawsleys. They would humiliate her – by inference if not in actual words. Her hands twisted in her lap. It was too much to ask of her.

'I cannot do it,' she reiterated. 'It may be very low-spirited of me but, please, I beg of you, do not press me on this matter.'

But Henry was adamant. 'Miss Rossall, your father was an educated, professional man. He and your mother have reared you with admirable gentility. You will be an asset at any dinner table. Besides, I need your presence to keep the proper balance of my guests. Without you, I cannot include Dr Jacobs. I would have to ask a couple – and that would leave just me and Miss Hawsley as the only two single people in the party, which would put her in an awkward position. Do you see my predicament?'

'I think Miss Hawsley would manage to rise above any unease such an arrangement might cause,' Bea said wryly.

'Perhaps so – but it would be discourteous of me to cause speculation. And there is no other single female whom I might invite without bringing about a similar predicament. Truly, you are essential to my table plan, Miss Rossall.'

Bea felt herself backed into a corner. 'But I have nothing suitable to wear,' she tried as a final plea. 'Only this dress.'

'Yes, you're right. Adequate though that dress is for dining *en famille*, it would be remiss of me to insist that you present yourself in company dressed in anything that would cause you to feel less than comfortable.'

Bea brightened. 'Then, I am excused from the dinner party?'

'No. The invitations have been dispatched. The dinner party will go ahead as planned.'

Bea's heart sank again. Why was he doing this to her? Was it because he wished to pursue Miss Hawsley? Was she to be cast in the role of an irrelevant diversion?

Henry pursed his lips and considered the options. Ah! 'Tell me, Miss Rossall, are you skilled in dressmaking?'

The question took her by surprise. 'Er ... sufficiently for my normal requirements, I believe. But you are surely not suggesting that I set to work to make a gown suitable for a dinner party? Apart from not having the spare time in which to do it, I wouldn't know where to start!'

'Not quite.' He smiled. 'I am thinking more along the lines of your adapting one of my late mother's gowns. You are of a similar build, I think. They are stored in a trunk in one of the upstairs rooms. I am sure there will be some that you may be able to adapt quite easily. Unfortunately, the bustle was in fashion in Mama's day but you should be able to remove those with Nanny Adams's help. She is quite skilled in the art of needlework and will be only too pleased to help you.'

Bea felt totally overwhelmed by the prospect but had to accept defeat on the issue since Mr Dearden refused to accept her pleas to excuse her.

The gowns were laid out for her perusal the following day. On close examination of them, she found that Mr Dearden was correct in one respect: the bustles could indeed be quite easily removed from the gowns, but the necklines were all embarrassingly low-cut, the puffed sleeves extremely short and the waists far too large.

Nanny Adams refused to be daunted. 'I'll take in the darts a bit to make the bodice fit and add some gathers at the waist of the skirt. A small peplum will hide the join and long gloves will make your arms feel less exposed. There are bound to be a few pairs in the trunk. I am sure Mrs Dearden had a pair to match every gown.'

By the time the gown had been altered to fit her Bea was feeling more accustomed to how it felt upon her. She had chosen one made of deep burgundy silk. The taken-in seams allowed the skirt to fall closely over her hips and, with the swaths of scooped layers removed from the skirt, the gown accentuated her slender form. Bea had to admit that it felt lovely against her skin and, without her spectacles and severe hairstyle, she would have drawn many an admiring glance from any gentleman with a discerning eye. That was exactly what she didn't want, however. So, although she agreed to have her hair in a slightly looser bun piled high upon her head, she replaced her spectacles with defiant determination.

The two girls were allowed to see her in her finery.

'You are like Cinderella in our Grimms' fairy story book!'

'And Nanny Adams is your fairy godmother!'

'So, there,' Nanny Adams said with a smile. 'You *shall* go to the ball – and there is no midnight curfew to change you back into your everyday clothes.'

When Bea descended the staircase soon after seven o'clock on the Saturday evening, Henry Dearden was of a similar opinion to his nieces. However, behind her cool reserve, he sensed her embarrassment and refrained from commenting upon her attractive appearance.

He ushered Bea into his sitting room. A few easy chairs were set in groups around the room with some straight-backed chairs interspersed among them but it was the grand piano that immediately drew Bea's glance.

'Oh, I didn't know you have a piano,' she exclaimed. 'Do you play?'

'A little – but not very well,' Mr Dearden confessed ruefully. 'Like many a schoolboy, I neglected to practise as much as I ought. What about you, Miss Rossall?'

'Yes. My mama taught me. She was an accomplished player. May I try it?'

'Of course.'

Bea lightly ran her fingers over the keys and was surprised to find it still in tune. She couldn't resist playing the opening bars of a melody that was one her favourites.

Before Henry could ask her its title, the drawing room door opened and Foster, the hired butler for the evening, announced, 'Mr and Mrs Alfred Hawsley and Miss Caroline Hawsley.'

Bea's heart sank. She had been hoping that the Hawsleys would not be the first to arrive. Mr Dearden immediately left her side and strode forward to greet his first guests.

Mrs Hawsley sailed towards him, cutting across his words of welcome. 'Now, you mustn't scold us for being unfashionably early, Mr Dearden. Your single status gives you such a disadvantage at social occasions such as this and I said to Mr Hawsley, "Mr Dearden has not thought to ask me to act as his hostess for the evening so we must go early and assure him that I am only too happy to serve in that capacity."' She playfully tapped his arm and smiled archly at him. 'We consider ourselves to be your closest friends and, under the circumstances, no one will think it to be in any way improper.'

'That is very kind of you, Mrs Hawsley,' Henry hastened to assure her. 'However, all I require of you is to grace my table with your delightful presence. Do step forward and ... Is something amiss, Miss Hawsley?'

That young lady was staring haughtily past him. 'You surely haven't asked your nieces' governess to act as your hostess, Mr Dearden?' she asked indignantly.

'Not at all. That would have been most improper on my part,' Henry said calmly, suppressing annoyance at her tone. 'Miss Rossall is—'

'Ah, then she need linger no longer now that we have arrived. I'm sure she has plenty of other things to do.' Miss

Hawsley spoke dismissively, adding sarcastically, 'I didn't know that piano tuning was one of her accomplishments. How extraordinary!'

'No, you mistake the situation!' Henry said curtly. 'Miss Rossall is here in the same capacity as yourself – as a guest.'

'A guest!' Mrs Hawsley exclaimed indignantly. 'Then I must assume that one of your other intended guests was unable to attend at the last minute, Mr Dearden. Why did you not let us know? I am sure any one of Caroline's many friends would have been only too happy to make up the numbers.'

Bea flushed at the arrogant contempt in her voice. How was she going to endure this evening? She held herself erect, refusing to allow her discomposure to show. Surely Mr Dearden must now see what a mistake this was?

'Not at all, Mrs Hawsley. As I said on the invitation, it is a gathering of friends. Now, why not take a seat over here until my other guests arrive.'

Mrs Hawsley eyed him coldly, then, with a curt toss of head, she turned her back on Bea and took the seat that was offered. Her husband and daughter followed suit. Bea remained standing by the piano, keeping at as great a distance from the Hawsleys as was socially polite.

Fortunately, Dr Jacobs was announced at that moment, shortly followed by Mr and Mrs Horace Cooke and Mr and Mrs Daniel Brownlow. As Mr Dearden quickly led the new arrivals forward, the arrival of Reverend and Mrs Pigot made the party complete. After the necessary introductions, Mrs Pigot rested her hand on Bea's arm. 'Come and sit by me whilst we drink our sherry, Miss Rossall, and we can get to know each other. You can tell me what it is like to be part of an inner-city church.'

Bea was thankful for a friendly overture and gladly sat by Mrs Pigot, who used her charm to put Bea at her ease; conversation with her was easy. Even so, she was relieved when Foster announced that dinner was ready to be served in the dining room. Mr Dearden had had the forethought to share his seating plan with her and she was thankful that, by deigning to honour the Hawsleys' long friendship with his family with seats by his side, he had thoughtfully placed her at the opposite end of the table, in between the Reverend Pigot and Mr Cooke with Mrs Brownlow opposite her.

Conversation flowed easily at the lower end of the table. Bea's knowledge of bellringing endeared her to the Brownlows and Mr Cooke was only too happy to explain to her the procedures involved in the manufacturing of paper.

'We must arrange a suitable time when you can bring Dearden's nieces to the papermill to see what goes on there,' he invited.

'You surprise me, Cooke, inviting delicate young girls to look around your factory,' Mr Hawsley commented, overhearing that part of the conversation. 'Factories are unhealthy places! I would not allow my daughter to step inside one.'

'I wouldn't wish to,' Miss Hawsley agreed with a shudder. 'One never knows what one might catch in such a place. Why, I can hardly bear to *look* at the women who work in factories, let alone stand near one to see what she is doing.'

'But you are delicately born, my dear,' Mrs Hawsley assured her. 'The lower classes do not have your sensibility.'

'But surely that is one of the reasons why we need to educate the lower classes, and where better to start than with the young girls who will be rearing the next generation?' Dr Jacobs pointed out mildly.

Mrs Hawsley sniffed derisively. 'What a waste of time!' she declared to all. 'It is a well-known fact that working-class children have no capacity for learning and young girls of the better classes of society such as our own are far too delicate. To try to educate them is so very dangerous! Why, everybody knows that female brains are not capable of much learning. It can cause them to overheat and can be fatal if taken to the extreme!'

Bea nearly choked on her soup. 'Oh, I assure you it is not so, Mrs Hawsley!' she managed to say more calmly than she felt. 'My father was determined to educate me as fully as he was able – and it is as well he did, or I would have been unable to support myself now that he is gone.'

Two red spots appeared in Mrs Hawsley's cheeks. She forced a smile to her lips but her eyes remained hostile. 'And, of course, having a baby to care for must have created difficulties for you, Miss Rossall? How fortunate that you were to find an employer with sufficient Christian charity to overlook such an ... indiscretion.'

Chapter 14

BEA PAUSED, A spoonful of soup half-raised to her lips. She lowered it down again, aware that all eyes were upon her. She was also aware that Mr Dearden, just within her range of vision at the head of the table, had lowered his spoon also, a thunderous expression upon his face. She feared the outrage would be made worse if he leaped to her defence.

She looked directly at Mrs Hawsley. 'Daisy isn't my natural daughter, Mrs Hawsley,' she managed to say calmly. 'She was placed in my care shortly before my father died – but I have every intention of adopting her as soon as I am able. Mr Dearden has very generously allowed me to keep her in my care whilst I am in his employment and I am very grateful for that.'

The silence hung heavily around the table. Bea felt too angry at having been targeted in such a way to look at the reactions of the other diners, but she kept her eyes levelly upon Mrs Hawsley, until that lady was forced to drop her gaze. Only then did she pick up her spoon again and declare quite brightly to her neighbour, 'This is delicious soup, is it not, Mr Cooke? Mrs Kellett has quite surpassed herself.'

And, with the subject changed, the tension around the table eased, though, later, as the gentlemen enjoyed a glass of port together, they admitted to one another that it had been the most stimulating dinner party they had known for quite some time and none wanted to linger over their port before returning to the drawing room to rejoin the ladies.

Bea was relieved when the gentlemen returned. The half-hour had seemed torturously long to her, even though the subject of Daisy's presence in the household had not been resurrected, thanks to Mrs Pigot's quelling glances in the Hawsleys' direction. With the full company back together, Bea refused to be drawn to express any more of her thoughts on education, and parried all attempts to break through her reserve. She did, however, consent to play the piano accompaniment to a number of popular songs and was thankful that the evening concluded in a harmonious way.

'There! That wasn't so bad, was it, Miss Rossall? You were a triumph!' Mr Dearden congratulated her when the last of the guests had departed.

Bea regarded him coolly. 'Really? I doubt Mrs Hawsley agrees with you.'

'Ah. What can I say ... except that I am sorry?' Mr Dearden apologized. 'Mrs Hawsley was exceedingly ill-mannered to bring up the subject of Daisy at the dinner table. You responded excellently. *I* was about to rebuke her most severely for her comment!'

Bea grimaced, thankful that she had at least prevented *that*. It would have destroyed him socially. She went to bed in a far happier frame of mind than she had expected.

What did it matter that the Hawsleys disliked her? They weren't her employers. Neither were they in control of her future. And the other guests hadn't shunned her, had they? She suddenly realized that the degradation she had suffered at the treatment dealt to her by Cyril Ackroyd was no longer important. Other people respected her and her ideas, and they had no intention of violating her.

As dinner drew to a close the following evening, Henry asked Bea if she had thought about going to see Dr Jacobs about her eyesight.

'Well, yes, I would like to do so,' she readily agreed. 'I wondered if I might take a couple of hours off duty on Saturday morning?'

Her words hit Henry hard. 'You haven't taken any time off since you came here, have you? Why didn't you tell me? I'm sure the other governesses took at least a half-day each week.' He heard the censure in his voice and immediately apologized. 'I'm sorry. I forget at times that you have had no experience in working for an employer. How about alternating your half day off on Saturday and Sunday afternoons, then we can be flexible if something unavoidable crops up?'

Bea agreed and, the next day, when she took the girls into town for the afternoon, notebooks in hand as they explored more of the town's streets, she made an appointment for a week the following Saturday. They returned in high spirits and added their findings to the street map of Horwich. Bea pinned the girls' drawings around the map, with lines of coloured wool leading to the exact position on the map.

Henry found his footsteps leading him to the schoolroom each day on his return from work, with the excuse of keeping track of the progress they were making. He made no excuses to himself for looking forward to the nightly conversation at the dinner table. He enjoyed Miss Rossall's company and hoped that that delight was reciprocated. When one of his work colleagues brought in two tickets that he could no longer use for a performance of Gilbert and Sullivan's operetta, *The Mikado*, Henry looked up in interest.

'At the Grand Theatre in Bolton? Which day?'

'Tomorrow evening. I know it's a bit short notice but our

eldest has gone down with mumps and the missus won't leave him. Are you interested, Dearden? I've seen you out and about with your young lady at various concerts. I'm sure she'd enjoy it.'

'I haven't exactly got a "young lady",' Henry responded, 'but, yes, I'll have the tickets. How much are they?'

The tickets and money were exchanged and Henry slipped the tickets into his jacket pocket, hoping Miss Rossall would accept the gesture as a peace-offering for his omission to make sure she had time off duty. Her reaction wasn't as he antici-pated. In fact, she looked shocked.

'I can't do that!' she exclaimed. 'You're my employer.'

'A very contrite one, who wishes to make amends,' he cajoled. 'Do accept – otherwise the tickets will be wasted. It is far too close to the performance for me to offer them elsewhere.'

With that point in mind, Bea eventually agreed.

It was a magical evening. They travelled in the comfort of a first-class carriage on the local train, then took a horse-drawn cab from the station to the theatre.

Once inside the auditorium, Bea was overcome with awe and admiration. The sheer height of the ornate domed ceiling drew her eyes up past the tiers of seating that swept around in an almost complete circle. Huge chandeliers hung above the auditorium, their twinkling lights sending shadows dancing around the walls as people were directed to their seats. Her eyes darted about, drinking in every detail so that she could describe the scene to the girls the following day.

Eventually the conductor raised his baton and a hush settled over the audience. The orchestra began to play and the heavy curtain rose to reveal the well-lit stage. The performance had begun. Its splendour took Bea's breath away. She leaned forward in her seat, her eyes hardly leaving the stage, her face enraptured.

Henry found himself delighting in watching her, realizing that her delight was infectious and had increased his own pleasure.

When the final curtain fell, Bea sighed in contentment. 'That was wonderful.'

Sleep was a long time in coming upon her that night. She basked in the afterglow of the pleasurable evening and how natural it had seemed to be there with her employer. He seemed to enjoy her company. Did that mean that he might invite her to accompany him to something similar again? Did she want him to? She had to admit that she did.

She wasn't aware how much her restored confidence showed in her demeanour but Mrs Kellett noticed it. She scowled and muttered her displeasure over her saucepans. 'She's 'eading fer a fall, that one is! But I'll be ready when her time comes.'

A deeper anger was mounting in another heart. Miss Hawsley couldn't believe what her friend had told her: that Henry Dearden had been seen in Bolton's Grand Theatre accompanied by someone other than herself! How dare he? How could he humiliate her so?

When she pressed for details of the woman's appearance, her credulity was stretched to its limit. There was only one woman among Henry Dearden's acquaintances who was tall and slender and wore quaint antiquated spectacles – the governess!

She was furious. He had taken that plain, impudent nonentity to the theatre without even offering the invitation to her! The fact that she had already been committed to a different event for that evening made no difference. She would have cancelled it without a second thought if Henry had extended the invitation to her! Heaven knows, she had been waiting long enough for such a personal invitation from him: one that didn't include her parents! Why did he think her parents had so often included him in *their* parties? People of her acquaintance were beginning to regard them as a couple and issued invitations to both of them when planning social events. How many of those people had now seen him escorting his nieces' plain governess? Even one would be too many! It was so humiliating!

She paced back and forth in the privacy of her bedroom, clenching and unclenching her hands. No! This upstart, this scheming woman, would not usurp her in his affections! She wouldn't allow it to happen! She would fight to reclaim him.

Her eyes narrowed. Who was she anyway, this plain nonentity? What lies had she spun to persuade him to employ her as his nieces' governess, even though she had a baby in her arms? A baby fathered by only heaven knew who!

Her heart almost stopped. Was it Henry Dearden's child? Surely he wouldn't be so indiscreet as to install his mistress as his nieces' governess? No, he had been taken in by whatever hard-luck story the governess had spun to him. He needed to be saved from his own gullibility. And she knew just how to do it!

First, she would write a carefully worded letter, anonymously, of course, to Mr Dearden's nieces' grandfather, then she would destroy the insufferable creature's credibility.

She recalled a conversation she had overheard at a recent dinner. Someone had hired a professional investigator to discover the background of a potential employee. She tapped her finger thoughtfully against her chin. She would tease the name of the man out of him without giving away her reason for doing so and would set the investigator to work on her behalf. She had no time to lose.

*

During dinner on the Friday evening Bea reminded Mr Dearden of her appointment with Dr Jacobs the following day.

'Yes. In fact, that will fit in beautifully. Miss Hawsley seems to have forgiven Winifred's episode with the flour and has asked us to accompany her on a visit to one of her friends this Saturday afternoon.'

Bea was surprised by the pang of dismay that hit her midriff. Surely she wasn't jealous? But she knew that she was. She was forced to admit to herself that at some undefined point in the past few weeks her feelings towards Mr Dearden had begun to change; a change so subtle that, had anyone challenged her about it, she would have instantly denied it.

But now she was faced with the dreadful realization: she was falling in love with him. Her senses felt vibrantly alert when he was near. She was aware of the warmth of his hand as he poured a glass of light table wine for her, and the slight scent of his skin when he held open the door so that she might precede him in or out of the dining room; and the way that a dimple appeared in his right cheek whenever he smiled, sending a strange fluttering sensation deep within her.

Even in the daytime when he was not there she was aware of the fragrance of the soap he used as she moved about the house, and if she had occasion to go into his library to borrow a book or a map the scent of the cigars he sometimes smoked was lingering in the air.

She hadn't meant to grow to love him. It wasn't something she had planned. It had come upon her slowly and had taken her unawares – and now it was too late. She loved him.

The realization shocked her. What was she to do about it? To reveal her feelings would probably bring about her instant dismissal – and *that* she couldn't bear to contemplate. She would never find a second employer willing to allow her to keep a baby under his roof. The thought made her genuinely feel quite ill. How could she have been so foolish?

Unconsciously she closed her eyes and took a deep breath to steady herself. No, he must never know of her feelings towards him.

'Is everything all right, Miss Rossall? You seem a little unwell?' Mr Dearden's voice broke into her reverie. She had no idea how long it was since he had spoken the words that had sent that disturbing shaft of self-knowledge to pierce her heart. Minutes? Seconds?

'No, no. I am fine,' she instinctively assured him, knowing that in reality she *wasn't* fine. 'Well, maybe a little headache,' she admitted. 'I really don't know.'

'It is exactly what I have suspected,' Mr Dearden declared.

Bea felt a stab of alarm. He suspected?

'You need a new prescription for your spectacles. It is as well that you have the appointment to see Dr Jacobs tomorrow afternoon,' he approved, misreading her alarm. 'And you needn't worry about what my nieces will be doing in your absence. They will be in excellent hands.'

Bea wasn't so sure of that. She knew that Winifred would not take kindly to Miss Hawsley's presence and hoped it wouldn't herald a set-back in Winifred's behaviour.

'I won't go!' Winifred declared defiantly when she was informed of the outing. 'It will be horrid! Why can't I come with you to see Dr Jacobs? I'd much prefer that.'

'Because that would upset your uncle. Miss Hawsley is a friend of his and he is looking forward to spending the day with her – and with you and Lily.'

'She hopes to marry him, but I hope he doesn't. She doesn't like us, does she, Lily?'

'No. She looks at us like this,' Lily agreed, crossing her eyes and looking down her nose.

It was so apt an imitation that Bea had to bite her inner cheeks to prevent a smile. 'It's up to your uncle to choose whom he marries,' she said firmly, twisting the pain in her own heart. 'So, make up your mind to enjoy the day, Winifred.'

Saturday arrived bright and clear. Mr Dearden had hired a carriage to take Miss Hawsley and the girls through nearby Rivington to Belmont, a small village on the edge of the moors where Miss Hawsley's friend lived. Bea watched them set off with some misgivings. Winifred had been too accepting; too demure in her manner. Neither did she like Miss Hawsley's proprietorial air over Mr Dearden, or his casual acceptance of it, but she knew she would have to grow accustomed to that if Winifred were right and Miss Hawsley did indeed intend him to be her husband.

Apart from her own feelings, she knew that Miss Hawsley was not right for him. He deserved a more caring person; someone who would love him and not try to dominate him.

The weather was so mild that she decided to take Daisy with her into town, glad to have the baby all to herself for an afternoon. Daffodils bloomed in the gardens of the terraced cottages leading down towards the town. The backdrop of the moors and Rivington Pike made Bea's heart almost sing for joy as she pushed the perambulator along the pavement. She loved it here. She must guard her position and not allow herself to even imagine that her relationship with Mr Dearden could ever be anything other than that of employer with employee.

Dr Jacobs' ophthalmic surgery was situated on Winter Hey Lane. Bea parked the perambulator in the small front garden and went inside, looking far more confident than she felt. How was she to convince Dr Jacobs that she needed to wear spectacles at all, let alone order a new pair – a pair with a much weaker lens?

The examination didn't take long. 'Although you have tried to convince me otherwise, Miss Rossall, your eyesight is almost perfect,' the puzzled Dr Jacobs remarked. 'Why do you want me to prescribe a new pair of spectacles for you?'

Bea twisted her hands together, her face red with embarrassment. 'It sounds so silly now, but I … well, I knew I would be a potential target for any man in the household where I gained employment, and so I decided to make myself as unattractive as I was able. Why are you smiling, Dr Jacobs? Do you find my predicament amusing? Or is it my vanity that amuses you? That I should think myself so beautiful as to be likely to make men desire me?'

'Neither, Miss Rossall. It is your belief that you made yourself unattractive that makes me smile. The spectacles you wear might give a first impression of plainness but that impression fades once a person has been in your presence for more than a minute.'

Bea glanced sharply at him. 'Do not make jest of me, Dr Jacobs. It is not something I did lightly. Deception is deception, whatever the motive – but now I know I did Mr Dearden an injustice. However, I am suffering from headaches and I cannot see clearly when I am reading and writing, except when the letters are written on the blackboard in large print. So, I would like you to make me a pair of spectacles that will suit my eyes.'

To Bea's relief, Dr Jacobs accepted her explanation and, although he admitted it was an unusual request, he agreed. 'I will have a pair made up for you, Miss Rossall. It won't take long. May I suggest that you call in for them on Wednesday afternoon?'

'Oh, yes.' She beamed at him. 'Goodbye, Dr Jacobs. Thank you so much.'

Her mind much relieved, Bea returned to Endmoor House by a circuitous route, enjoying the freedom of being out with Daisy on her own. When Daisy woke up, Bea pushed back the hood and propped the pillow behind her.

'There, that's better. How's my little baby enjoying being out in the sunshine?'

Daisy cooed at the sound of her voice and Bea smiled. 'When we get home we can play for a while. Won't that be nice? Just you and me and Nanny Adams.'

But when they eventually approached Endmoor House she could see a carriage drawing up by the gate. At first she thought Mr Dearden had brought the children back early and her heart sank. What had Winifred done now? However, when she saw that the descending passenger was an elderly gentleman wearing a warm frock-coat and a tall hat, she realized her mistake. She quickened her pace and was only a few yards away when he went through the gateway. As he turned to close the gate behind him, she smiled a greeting.

'Good afternoon, sir. Would you be so kind as to hold open the gate for me, please? It's so difficult to manoeuvre this perambulator through on my own. Thank you,' she added as he did as she requested.

He glowered at her as he stepped back a little to allow her to push the large perambulator through the gateway. Undeterred, she smiled at him. 'Are you wishing to see Mr Dearden, sir? I'm afraid he isn't in at the moment. Maybe I can be of assistance to you?'

'And you are?' he asked coolly.

Bea smiled, understanding his reticence. From his dress and demeanour he was obviously a gentleman, and her garb was hardly that of his equal. 'My name is Beatrice Rossall. I am Mr Dearden's nieces' governess.'

'Are you, indeed?'

Bea felt a little nonplussed by the coldness of his tone but courtesy persuaded her to add, 'May I ask your name, sir? I am sure Mr Dearden will be sorry to have missed you.'

The man's response came swift with restrained anger. 'Mr Dearden will be even sorrier when he sees me and is forced to explain why he has employed an unmarried woman with an illegitimate child to be my granddaughters' governess.'

Bea was shocked by his vehemence. He was the girls' grandfather? Then his name was Sharrock or something like that. No, it was Sharratt. Albert Sharratt, a shoe-factory owner. And his wife was an invalid – wasn't that what Nanny Adams had said when she explained why they were unable to look after their granddaughters when their daughter died?

Mr Sharratt's slur on her character penetrated belatedly. She tilted her chin high, deliberately holding his glare. 'Daisy is not my child in the way that you are suggesting, Mr Sharratt,' she denied with quiet dignity. 'But I do consider myself to be Daisy's unofficial guardian. Her mother died in childbirth whilst under the protection of my father, the late Reverend Rossall. Mr Dearden is in full possession of the facts of Daisy's birth. If my appointment here disturbs you in any way, you must take it up with Mr Dearden on his return.'

'Oh, I will, Miss Rossall, I will. And I will demand your instant dismissal. How dare you have the effrontery to bring one of Dearden's bastards here?'

Chapter 15

B EA WAS TAKEN aback by both his sense of outrage and his mistaken assumption. Her face flared with heat.

'No, no. You are mistaken, sir. I thought the same but I was wrong. Mr Dearden is not Daisy's father. He assures me he has never met Elsie Brindle, Daisy's mother – and I believe him.'

Mr Sharratt laughed harshly. 'I am not talking of Mr *Henry* Dearden. I am talking of my no-good son-in-law, *Frederick* Dearden, Miss Rossall. Unless I am very mistaken, he is the father of this child – and I will not allow my granddaughters to be shamed by her acceptance in this household!'

Bea stared at him aghast. 'No, no, you are wrong, sir. Mr Frederick Dearden had long gone to America, before Daisy was born. She is not yet eight months old. I was there at her birth. I have accepted that we will never know who her father is. That is why I have decided to regard her as my own child. I am all she has got.'

'Your philanthropy is commendable, Miss Rossall, but it is you who are mistaken. That child is a Dearden through and through. She is the image of Winifred at the same age and, as she gets older, the likeness will be more and more apparent to anyone who sees them together. She represents the final degradation that caused my daughter to take her own life.

Now, if you will allow me access into Mr Dearden's house, I will await his return.'

The girls' mother had taken her own life? Somehow she had heard of Daisy's birth and believed her husband to have sired her? It didn't make sense. Mr Dearden had said his sister-in-law had died nearly a year ago, long before Daisy had been born – and Freddie had already departed for America, hadn't he? Had he not been gone for as long as she supposed? Daisy had been small at birth and they had all thought she had been born prematurely – but if she had been full-term, her conception could have been earlier, whilst Frederick was still in England.

Shaken by Mr Sharratt's revelation, Bea pushed the perambulator around to the back of the house, letting Mrs Kellett know of the presence of the visitor and ordering refreshments for him before she hurried upstairs to deposit Daisy with Nanny Adams. She recalled the nanny's comments on Daisy's similarity to Winifred when they had first arrived in the household, comments she had disregarded as an elderly lady's confused memory. Had Nanny Adams been correct after all?

Another thought struck her forcibly. Had Mr Dearden also seen the family likeness? Had he known all along that his brother was Daisy's father? Why had he not shared his knowledge with her? Instead, he had denied her the solace of knowing Daisy's parentage. Didn't he trust her?

After leaving Daisy with Nanny Adams, Bea felt duty-bound to return downstairs to offer some hospitality to Mr Sharratt. However, when she was halfway down the stairs, she was relieved to see Mr Dearden and the two girls entering through the front door. Winifred was scowling and Mr Dearden ordered her upstairs.

'And you too, Lily. Yes, I know you weren't as naughty as Winifred but I can see from the carriage outside that we have a visitor. Ah, Miss Rossall, perhaps you can enlighten me as to who that is?'

Winifred ran up the stairs, brushing past Bea with her head down. Lily followed her more slowly and Bea allowed her to pass without hindering her. There were questions she needed to clear up with Mr Dearden – but not just now.

'It is Mr Sharratt, the girls' grandfather, Mr Dearden. He is in the drawing room.' She had kept her voice level and controlled, but now she paused and looked directly into his eyes as she added, 'He arrived as I was coming back to the house with Daisy. He was somewhat perturbed to see her and expressed his feelings most vociferously.'

Bea was pleased to note that Mr Dearden looked somewhat guilty at that – and so he ought. However, she didn't want to keep him from his visitor, so she simply added, 'I have asked Mrs Kellett to provide him with refreshments. I will check to see if they have been served.'

She turned abruptly and made her way to the kitchen, leaving Mr Dearden to take in what she had said and decide on his course of action. Not that he had much choice. When Bea looked over her shoulder before slipping through into the back of house, he was already entering the drawing room and greeting their visitor. Much as she would have loved to over-hear what was said, she knew she must restrain her curiosity.

Mrs Kellett eyed her with some satisfied malice. 'Mr Sharratt'll soon sort you out, miss,' she gloated. 'Pack you off to where you came from like as not. He's a gentleman and knows what's right and what's wrong, an' if he's staying for dinner, it'll be the gentlemen only. You'll be 'avin' yours in the nursery wi' the others.'

'No, I will have my dinner on a tray in my room, Mrs Kellett,' Bea said calmly. 'I will let you know at what time, when we know whether or not Mr Sharratt is staying to dinner. Ah, I can see the refreshments are ready. Excellent. Come, Gertie; put on a clean apron and push the trolley into the drawing room. Thank you, Mrs Kellett. It looks very nice.'

Bea turned about and left the kitchen, waiting until Gertie appeared with the trolley before proceeding ahead of her towards the drawing room. She could hear raised voices.

'No, I will not dismiss her,' Mr Dearden was declaring forcefully. 'Miss Rossall is an excellent teacher and is drawing out both Winifred and Lily's capabilities. She is a respectable woman, the daughter of a clergyman and is by far the best governess your granddaughters have had whilst they have been in my care.'

'Then that bastard child must go! I will not have my granddaughters contaminated by her!' Mr Sharratt returned just as forcefully.

'There is no contamination! Daisy is just a baby. The girls are enjoying helping to look after her. Besides, Miss Rossall will never agree to stay without Daisy. And if she *is* my brother's child, then he must be persuaded to make some provision for her.'

'*If* she is his child? Are you blind, man? Of course she is his child – along with half a dozen others scattered around the county! Are you going to take them all under your roof? I think not!'

Bea rapped loudly upon the door. The voices hushed immediately and she beckoned to Gertie to take the trolley into the room. She felt too agitated to go to the nursery and so withdrew to her room, where she paced restlessly up and down, wondering what would be the outcome of the battle of wills downstairs. Half an hour later there was a knock on her door. When she opened it, her employer stood before her, his nieces at his side.

'Miss Rossall, Mr Sharratt has asked to speak to you and his granddaughters. If you will take them along to the schoolroom, I will bring him to meet you there. He will want to see some written pieces of their work.' His expression showed no indication that anything untoward had taken place in the drawing room, for which Bea was thankful.

The girls were excited and, although Winifred was a little subdued, she joined with Lily to select some of her pieces of written work, some drawings and pages of sums set out far more neatly than they had been when Bea first took over their schooling.

The girls were standing quietly by Bea's side, but when the door opened and their grandfather stepped into the schoolroom both girls cried out, 'Grandfather!' and ran towards him. He stooped down and hugged them to his side, brushing the tops of their heads with his bewhiskered lips. Bea was glad to see the familial affection and found herself relaxing somewhat. Whatever had been thrashed out downstairs was obviously not going to intrude into Mr Sharratt's relationship with his granddaughters.

He examined the pieces of work the girls eagerly pushed into his hands, giving praise in equal measure to both girls, finding something positive to say about each piece. His interest in the enlarged map of Horwich which was hung on the wall seemed to be genuine.

'This is your doing, is it, Miss Rossall?' he asked, turning to her directly for the first time since Mr Dearden had officially introduced her.

'I instigated the project and help a little whenever necessary,' she admitted. 'It is work in progress, as you can see. We make visits into town a couple of times each week and add drawings of our observations on our return. Most of it is Winifred's handiwork but Lily has also contributed towards it.'

'I like drawing, Grandfather,' Winifred told him. 'Miss Rossall says that, when I grow up, I might get a job in a drawing office, like Uncle Henry, if I work hard enough.'

Mr Sharratt raised his eyes to meet with Bea's over the heads of his granddaughters. Although not exactly full of bonhomie towards her, his glance held none of his former rancour. 'Then we must hope that Miss Rossall knows what she is talking about. I cannot fault your work, Miss Rossall. On other matters I am persuaded to hold my judgement.'

Bea nodded briefly, to acknowledge his magnanimity in being willing to step down from his earlier antagonism towards her. 'I am enjoying my work here and find your grand-daughters a delight to teach, Mr Sharratt.'

Mr Sharratt returned his interest to Winifred and Lily and Bea felt herself dismissed. She retreated into the background, idly touching and rearranging various artefacts in the school-room. She was startled to sense a presence standing close behind her and half-turned to find Mr Dearden towering over her, feigning interest in a piece of writing pinned to the wall.

'We will talk later, over dinner,' he murmured.

'We will not!' she hissed. 'I have decided to eat in my room from now on.' When had she decided that? she wondered, knowing instantly that it was when she realized that Mr Dearden had chosen to keep her in ignorance about his brother's betrayal of both his wife and Elsie Brindle. How could she eat and converse with someone who accorded her such scant respect?

'You will dine with me as usual!' he murmured, just as forcefully. 'After Mr Sharratt has returned to Blackburn to dine with his wife. I will inform Mrs Kellett of our later time.'

Bea had no option but to agree, but she was determined to have her say.

She was quiet but civil on entering the dining room, waiting until Gertie left the room before speaking of her disquiet. When Mr Dearden reached out to lift the lid from the meat platter, Bea placed her hand on top of his, forcing it down again.

'I have no appetite for eating, Mr Dearden,' she said coolly. 'I am too distressed by your decision to keep me in ignorance of Daisy's true parentage. You *knew* your brother was responsible for ... for Daisy's conception – and its consequences for Elsie Brindle – and yet you chose to keep that information to yourself, letting me believe that all avenues for discovering the name of Daisy's father were closed for ever. Did you hope I would quietly go away and that no one would ever know of your brother's dishonourable behaviour?'

'If that had been my prime objective, I would hardly have engaged you to be my nieces' governess, would I?' Mr Dearden replied reasonably. 'I am sorry to have deceived you. I ... I thought it best at the time. After all, I didn't know you. I didn't know your character. Nor whether you hoped for some monetary payments for your silence – and neither ...' He held up his hand, as Bea made a move to defend her character. 'No, let me speak. I was about to say that, at that point, neither did I know for certain whether Freddie is indeed Daisy's father.'

Bea accepted the truth of that. 'But, afterwards, after you had got to know that I wasn't considering anything so abhorrent as blackmail – and after you had had time to get to know Daisy, surely you saw the family likeness? Nanny Adams commented on it, but I just assumed she was feeling muddled.

Couldn't you have eased my burden then and made some acknowledgement that I hadn't acted too impulsively in bring Daisy here? I wouldn't have made any demands on you.'

Her voice broke a little and Henry reached out to touch her arm. 'I wished many a time that I might, but I wasn't sure what you would do, and I felt I needed to have Freddie's admission of guilt before I could offer any recompense on his behalf.'

Bea fell silent. She could understand his dilemma but still felt demeaned by his lack of trust. 'So, what happens now? Now that we know Freddie *is* Daisy's father? Mr Sharratt isn't happy about her being brought up alongside his granddaughters? Do you want us to leave?' She knew what she had overheard but needed to be sure it was still Mr Dearden's intention.

'I want us to continue as we have been doing so far, at least until I hear from Freddie.' He spread out his hands apologetically. 'I have not yet had a reply from him. Maybe my letter has not yet reached him.'

'Or maybe he is staying out of the way?'

Mr Dearden nodded. 'That is always possible. Freddie always did choose the easy way out of any unpleasant situation – but he will have to return home at some point in the future. I have already cancelled his banking draft. He will come home when he realizes his source of funding has run dry.'

'Surely he will want to see Winifred and Lily? And, what about his wife? Does he not yet know of her death?'

Mr Dearden sighed. 'Freddie carries his responsibilities as a father very lightly, I'm afraid. Not that he would ever see the girls truly neglected – but he is happy to leave them in my care. As to whether he yet knows of Mary's death? We will only know the answer to that when he deigns to reply to my letter. Until then, we must assume that he doesn't.'

Bea chewed her lower lip. 'Mr Sharratt said that she had taken her own life; that she knew about Daisy. But, how could she? Mrs Martland cast Elsie out. I doubt she passed on Elsie's accusation to your brother's wife.'

Henry met her eyes sombrely. 'It is a sad tale. Mr Sharratt has now told me that Mary was indeed expecting another baby … and, aware of Freddie's frequent affairs, she couldn't face having another child. That must be what Winifred overheard: Mary telling her parents of the coming baby. Tragically, neither Mr nor Mrs Sharratt suspected that Mary felt desperate enough to take her own life. I beg you not to breathe a word of any of this to anyone. The girls have enough to come to terms with, without adding that to the list.'

Bea agreed but added, 'I suspect some idea of it has already occurred to Winifred.'

'Maybe. She was certainly a very troubled girl when first she came here.' He smiled, easing the tension between them, reaching out once more to remove the lid from the meat salver and beginning to place some slices of excellent roast beef on to a plate. 'It is thanks to you, Miss Rossall, that she is now much happier and I told Mr Sharratt so.' He passed the plate to her, smiling in a teasing manner. 'I really did fight your corner, Miss Rossall and so I hope you aren't thinking that the only course of action for you is to leave.'

Bea dropped her glance, embarrassed by his praise, and by the fact that she had overheard his strong defence of her. 'No, I am not thinking of leaving, Mr Dearden. I must at least wait until we know of your brother's reaction to Daisy and whether he intends to support her in any way. I cannot afford to stand upon any principles of indignation or pique against him.' She paused, then asked curiously, 'What exactly brought Mr Sharratt here to visit you today? If he had let you know in advance, you would not have taken the girls out.'

Henry frowned. 'He said it was in response to a letter ... written by a 'well-wisher'. Someone who thought it his or her duty to inform him of the 'unsavoury state' of my household. I wonder who that could be? It is a little unsettling to realize that an outsider sees fit to act in that way.'

Bea agreed but could offer no suggestions – none that she cared to mention, anyway.

Chapter 16

WHEN BEA QUERIED the nature of Winifred's misbehaviour, Mr Dearden said that she had been very rude to Miss Hawsley and was to be denied any access to her drawing board for a week as a punishment.

'Very well,' Bea agreed, adding, 'though I presume she may draw when it is part of a lesson?'

'You will have to use your own judgement on that, Miss Rossall,' Mr Dearden responded shortly. 'Winifred must not be allowed to think she can get away with such rude behaviour. You will pack away the drawing board tomorrow afternoon.'

Bea wondered whether he had deliberately chosen that Winifred's punishment should take effect after church, rather than before it. However, she was thankful that it was so, since Winifred did make an effort to be civil to Miss Hawsley before and after the morning service, even though she rolled her eyes and made a sickly face whenever Miss Hawsley laid her hand possessively on Mr Dearden's arm and spoke in a sugary-sweet manner to him.

When told later of the punishment, Winifred was unrepentant. 'I don't care. Why should I be nice to her when I know very well she hates us and is only pretending to like us to make Uncle Henry think she is a nice person. Which she isn't. She told me Uncle Henry is thinking of sending me away to school, but I bet it's *her* idea.'

Bea chose not to respond. She knew Winifred's assessment of Miss Hawsley was probably correct. She rearranged a few lesson plans and the incident passed by.

Mr Dearden had dinner elsewhere on two evenings that week and Bea wondered whether he was tiring of sharing his time at dinner with her. She was therefore surprised when he invited her to accompany him to a performance by the Railway Works Prize Brass Band at the Mechanics' Institute on the Thursday evening. Bea again pondered on the wisdom of becoming socially involved with her employer but her doubts were outweighed both by Mr Dearden's prosaic manner as he issued the invitation and by the prospect of the musical entertainment – and she did so want to go. After all, it was simply an evening's entertainment; nothing more.

Wearing her new spectacles, Bea was able to enjoy the evening without being distracted by blurred vision. The hall was comfortably filled and, during the interval, Mr Dearden introduced her to a number of his work colleagues, all of whom were very pleasant towards her. She enjoyed the concert and, it was no use denying it, she enjoyed being there with Mr Dearden. In spite of his failure to share his suspicions of Daisy's parentage with her, his close presence caused her to feel all sorts of emotions that had hitherto passed her by. She felt feminine and protected. It was only in the privacy of her room at night, when she allowed herself the luxury of going over every moment she had spent in his company, that she admitted to herself how dear he had become to her.

Oh, she knew it was a hopeless love. Nothing could ever come of it, especially if Miss Hawsley had her way and managed to entrap him, but she couldn't help it. She decided that she must simply treasure every day she remained in his household and do her best to repay his kindness towards her by educating his nieces to the best of her ability.

Miss Hawsley's fury knew no bounds when an acquaintance took delight in telling her that once again Mr Dearden had escorted the governess to the band concert. All her efforts to ingratiate herself with his dreadful nieces seemed to be having no effect whatsoever. Neither did the fact that they were so often invited to the same dinner function and generally seated in close proximity to each other. Was he so naïve that he thought it simply happened by chance? Really! How obtuse could the man be? Did he not realize that however skilled he was in the railway works drawing office, he was merely a middle-class man who was socially sought after because of *her* connections, not because of *his*?

Of course, his lack of pretension was part of his attraction for her. He wasn't shallow like so many other gentlemen in her social circle. Once he was brought to the point of commitment, he would remain true. He wouldn't lead her up the garden path and expect to have the liberty of having affairs with whoever else took his fancy – though she wondered whether he might, after a while, prove to be a little too dull? But then, as long as she was discreet, he probably wouldn't even notice if her attentions wandered a little. And she *did* know how to be discreet. No whispers circulated about her little forays into the exciting twilight world she had discovered and found to be so necessary to her; however, she needed a cloak of respectability and Henry Dearden was the man to provide it! She was not going to let that plain, prissy nonentity of a governess get in the way of her plans.

Strangely, her anonymous letter to Albert Sharratt hadn't

brought about the removal of her adversary. Had it somehow become lost in the post? Maybe she should write again, adding a few more vaguely worded insinuations to elicit a better response? If she heard nothing soon from the shifty-eyed Turnbull, whom she had hired to ferret around for any unsavoury information about Miss Goody-goody Rossall in Salford, she would certainly do so!

It was her guess that the so-called Reverend Rossall didn't even exist! Why, anyone could make up such a semi-respectable background if they then moved to live in another area! Why else would the woman bring her illegitimate child here to Horwich, when there were surely richer pickings elsewhere? No, there was something unsavoury in the woman's background, and when she discovered what it was Miss Rossall's days at Endmoor House would be numbered. Henry would turn to her, Caroline Hawsley, for the restoration of his self-esteem, and she would then make sure that no one else had the opportunity to steal her intended husband from under her nose!

Two days later, the much-awaited message from Sidney Turnbull was delivered to her friend, Miss Ingham who, dutifully and unsuspectingly, passed it on. Miss Ingham's pretty face flushed excitedly at being party to such a romantic undertaking. 'Oh, to think you have a secret admirer, Caroline! It must be so thrilling! Are you really going to meet him without telling your mama and papa?'

'Of course. Tomorrow afternoon, you and I will travel together to Bolton and I will meet my "friend", as arranged, in the Chadwick Museum in Queens Park, whilst you stroll around the park until I am ready to meet you – and not a word to anyone!'

The following day Miss Hawsley's nose wrinkled in distaste when she entered the museum and saw the carelessly dressed man awaiting her. She wore a heavy veil over her face and sincerely hoped that nobody there knew her well enough to recognize her. She made no move to touch the far-from-clean hand he extended towards her. Instead, she turned away from him and peered with exaggerated interest at the stuffed body of a rabbit, cruelly caught in the talons of a bird of prey.

'Tell me quietly what you have learned, Turnbull, whilst you scrutinize this disgusting tableau. You have no need to look at me as you speak and do not speak my name. I have no wish to draw attention to ourselves.'

'Right yer are, miss. Well, fer a start, yer'll be disappointed to learn that the young lady's father was indeed a vicar and a very respected one at that.'

Disappointment surged through her. 'Damn! I was sure she was lying! What about her child? What did you discover with regards to that?'

'Ah, now, that's what I know will interest you, miss! I met a man who knew the family well. A respected member of the parochial church council. You'll be interested in what he had to say about the strait-laced daughter of the vicar! Had a babby, she did – though some of the folks I talked to reckoned it weren't 'ers. 'Owever, the gentleman I spoke of assured me as it was. Disgraced she was, and had to run away. 'E' said as 'ow 'e's been lookin' fer 'er an' is willin' to tek 'er in – but not with the babby. It's not 'is, yer see, an' 'e won't tek on somebody else's bastard, not fer love nor money. Not that there's much "*love*" in what he wants her for, if yer get me meanin'!' He laughed harshly, causing Miss Hawsley to glance around in alarm.

'Hush, man! How do I get in touch with him, this man you spoke to? Did you get his postal address, as I suggested?'

'I did, miss, an' yer shall 'ave it as soon as yer pays me the necessary.'

Miss Hawsley shuddered at the sight of his extended grubby hand, but reached into the reticule that hung on her arm. Aware that the man was eyeing it greedily, she swiftly withdrew a small envelope. 'This is all I brought with me, so don't even attempt to ask for more,' she said haughtily, holding it in front of him. She pulled it back sharply when he reached out to take it. 'The address, please.'

The exchange made, the two unlikely conspirators parted company and, after fleeting glances in a number of groundfloor rooms, Miss Hawsley left the building on her own and eventually rejoined her friend, silently mulling over her next move in the sequence of events she was planning.

One Sunday, just over a week later, Henry surprised Miss Rossall by passing on an invitation which he had been given as he passed the time of day with the Hawsleys after morning church, conscious that Miss Rossall and his nieces were enjoying a much more lively conversation with Mr and Mrs Greenhalgh and their daughter Eliza. He waited until they were walking back up Church Street, when Winifred and Lily had skipped ahead of them.

Miss Rossall's face lost all colour as she halted abruptly and turned to face him. 'An invitation to dine? From the Hawsleys? Surely you are mistaken?' At least, she hoped he was! His smiling response killed all hope of that.

'No, I am not mistaken. Mrs Hawsley said how well you seem to have settled into the community and to have been accepted by some members of society, and that she saw no reason to maintain a distance from you.'

Bea was appalled. 'That is very condescending of her. You surely don't expect me to accept the invitation?'

'I have already done so on your behalf. It must have been

very difficult for her to climb down from her former position on the matter and I am sure you will see fit to forgive her manner of issuing the invitation.'

Bea felt her face flushing at his implied criticism. His voice held a considerable measure of warmth, and when she raised her eyes to his they held an expression of tenderness, not condemnation. It was she who looked away first. 'You are right. I am sorry to judge her so harshly. Very well, I will accompany you to dine with them, though I cannot say I do so with an easy heart. When is it to be?'

They resumed their walk as Henry replied. 'A week on Tuesday, the twenty-fourth of May. How the year is passing by. Summer will be upon us soon.'

Bea realized that he was seeking to alleviate her agitation by speaking of mundane matters, but she knew she would not feel at ease until the dinner date was behind her.

The day came round all too quickly. Bea wished that some minor inconvenience might overcome her, such as a heavy cold or an upset stomach, but no such escape route was offered to her. She dressed in another of Mr Dearden's mother's altered gowns. Its dark-gold silk was quite becoming, even though its over-large puffed sleeves did date it from an earlier era. Nanny Adams managed to take out some of the fullness of the sleeves and fashioned a silk rose for Bea to wear in her hair; also persuading her at the last minute to coil the fullness of her hair on top of her head instead of drawing it back into its more usual severe style. Standing over Bea as she sat on a stool in front of her dressing-table mirror, Nanny also tweaked out a few curls at the front and fluffed them over Bea's forehead.

'There, that's much better, my girl,' she said with satisfaction as she stepped back to view her handiwork. 'No need for pads in *your* hair; it's full enough on its own. You look quite attractive when you choose to do so, my dear. And don't go pulling it back tight the minute you leave this room, 'cause there isn't time to start all over again.'

Bea surveyed her reflection with a mixture of feelings. The image staring back at her *was* attractive. She supposed it might boost her confidence a little to know she could hold a candle to Miss Hawsley and it was with some reluctance that she picked up her spectacles and placed them back on to the bridge of her nose.

'Pity about them, too.' Nanny Adams voiced her thoughts. 'I suppose you couldn't leave them off for tonight?'

'Unfortunately, no.' Bea was surprised to note that her words expressed her true feelings. What a ridiculous rod for her own back she had made! At least this new pair didn't give her headaches and blurred vision and, being rimless, were less obtrusive. But, no, they were still her safeguard from unwanted attentions. Even from Mr Dearden, whom only in her dreams could she allow the liberty of his gently removing them from her face; a notion that was reinforced a few minutes later when she descended to staircase to the hall, where Mr Dearden was waiting. A delighted smile lit his face as he took in her appearance and he offered his crooked arm with a gallant half-bow.

'Your carriage awaits you, ma'am,' he quipped, the sparkle in his eyes bringing a faint blush to Bea's cheeks. He looked very smart in his tail coat with its satin lapels and the narrow-cut trousers. His plain white shirt with its straight standing three-inch high collar and his single-breasted waistcoat were immaculate, as was the neat bow tie.

Bea suspected a similar light of approval shone from her eyes, too, and she cast them down swiftly in order to hide it.

The carriage driver tipped his hat to Bea. Mr Dearden held

out his gloved hand and Bea placed her fingers into it. Even through the thin fabric of her silk gloves, she sensed she could feel the heat of his hand and tiny bursts of fire spiralled round her body. She looked at him from under her lashes as he handed her up into the carriage. Did he feel it too? She wasn't sure, though he seemed to be startled by something – but he shook his hand impatiently and laughed as he climbed up beside her.

'A touch of pins and needles,' he quipped. 'Drive on, Tom.'

It was about half a mile further along Chorley Old Road towards Bolton to the Hawsleys' house and, in spite of the moderate temperature of the late May evening, Bea was thankful for the complementary flared cape she wore over her shoulders. She felt tense and no amount of good humour or teasing from Mr Dearden could release her from it. All she longed for was the end of the evening. Four hours – that was all she had to endure.

It was a large double-fronted house with a sweeping driveway and a semicircular arc of three steps leading up to the front door. A maid answered Mr Dearden's tug of the bell pull and took Bea's cape and Mr Dearden's black-silk top hat.

'Mr and Mrs Hawsley and their other guest are awaiting you in the drawing room, sir, miss,' she said, placing the cape and hat on a side table, next to a larger hat of similar design. 'If you'll follow me.'

So, there was just one other male visitor was there? Bea supposed, wondering to whom the honour had been extended. She hoped it might be Dr Jacobs. He was a pleasant young man, though she couldn't imagine him being a candidate for Miss Hawsley's affections. Nor, she suspected, would her parents wish to fling her into such a kind-natured gentleman's path.

A murmur of voices sounded through the doorway as the maid opened the door and some latent instinct seemed to warn her of danger, causing her heart to begin to beat rapidly. Bea later wondered why she hadn't turned and run immediately – but she shook the premonition away, telling herself not to be so fanciful.

She nervously entered the drawing room, still unprepared for the shock that awaited her. The assembled group were seated in a wide arc around the glowing fire, as if in a specially arranged tableau, Bea reflected later. Mr and Mrs Hawsley were on separate chairs, on opposite sides of the fireplace; Miss Hawsley and the unknown male guest were on two separate two-seater sofas, again on opposite sides of the fire, the unknown guest with his back towards the door. Each held a glass of sherry in one hand as they conversed. That voice? Surely she knew its tones?

Mrs Hawsley rose to her feet first, closely followed by her husband. 'Ah, Mr Dearden. There you are. How delightful. And Miss Rossall, too. Do come and join us.'

Still unaware of what lay before her, Bea stepped forward, trying to force the muscles of her face to relax into a recipro-cating smile. It was only as the male guest rose from his seat and turned towards her that Bea's steps halted and her body froze. A loud roaring sound seemed to fill her head as Mrs Hawsley's voice continued with false sweetness. 'I believe you are acquainted with Mr Ackroyd, Miss Rossall?'

Chapter 17

BEA FELT AS if she were in the midst of a nightmare. She clutched at Mr Dearden's arm. How could Mr Ackroyd have found out where she was? Or was he already connected to the Hawsleys – and this meeting was an unplanned coincidence? She struggled to regain her composure, wishing she could deny all knowledge of him – but the satisfied glint in the Hawsleys' eyes revealed they knew that that was not so! What exactly *did* they know? Surely not the whole degrading truth! No, Ackroyd would not have admitted that. She tried to push down her fear.

'Mr Ackroyd is a businessman in what was my father's parish,' she said tonelessly, shrinking closer to Mr Dearden. She felt as though her legs were about to give way beneath her and she needed to lean against him.

'Oh, come, Miss Rossall, do not be so reticent!' Miss Hawsley trilled. 'You are among friends!' She glanced coyly at the others present and said conspiratorially, 'Mr Ackroyd has already hinted at a much closer interest in Miss Rossall, haven't you, Mr Ackroyd? A relationship that Miss Rossall cruelly brought to an end – though he is far too much the gentleman to disclose the details.'

Mr Ackroyd inclined his head gravely. 'Indeed, I have a great fondness for her, but Miss Rossall likes to play her little games, don't you, my dear?'

Bea's face flamed. How dare he put such a slur on her character! She straightened her spine and met his gaze coldly. 'I
rarely dissemble, Mr Ackroyd and I have *never* played games
with you.'

A flicker of anger in Mr Ackroyd's eyes was swiftly banished
and he gravely clasped his hands over his heart. 'Do not say so,
Miss Rossall, for that means that you meant every cruel word.'

Henry felt bewildered by what was happening. The
Hawsleys and their guest, this Ackroyd fellow, as mean-looking
an individual as ever he had clapped eyes on, seemed to be
acting out a prearranged scene, the words of which, although
innocent enough in themselves, seemed to imply something not
quite so innocent – and their effect on Miss Rossall was
alarming. He suspected that, if he were not there by her side,
she would crumple to the ground.

'Do let's be seated,' Mrs Hawsley was saying. 'A glass of
sherry, Miss Rossall? You seem quite pale.' She nodded her
head towards Mr Hawsley, indicating the decanter of sherry
that stood on a small table by his chair.

As she spoke, the Hawsleys resumed their seats and Henry
could see at a glance that the place Mrs Hawsley had in mind
for Miss Rossall was the spare half of the two-seater sofa that
Ackroyd had vacated and was now hovering by until the three
ladies were seated. He swiftly placed his hand over Miss
Rossall's hand, the hand that was still gripping tightly to his
left arm. He sensed panic in her rigid stance and spoke as
warmly as he could.

'Yes, you are shivering, Miss Rossall. I regret ordering the
open carriage for our journey. I had thought the air warmer
than it actually is. Come and warm yourself by the fire before
you sit down.' He led her towards the fire and disengaged her
hand from his arm, helping her to extend her hands towards

the dancing flames. He glanced back towards the sofa. Ackroyd was still standing, ready to claim his place by Miss Rossall's side once she was seated. Henry turned and drew Miss Rossall towards the sofa, deliberately forcing Ackroyd to step away as he did so. He knew that Miss Hawsley was trying to catch his eye to beckon him to sit beside her but he had no intention whatever of allowing that fellow to sit in close proximity to Miss Rossall. She seemed to both loathe and fear him.

'Sit here, Miss Rossall.' He lowered his voice as he added, 'You will be quite safe.' Her fingers gripped his hand as she seated herself and, flicking back the tails of his coat, Henry sank down beside her, pretending not to notice Ackroyd's fury. He beamed around. 'Well, this is nice and cosy. I am sure Miss Rossall will soon be feeling warmed again.'

Bea wasn't sure how she got through that dreadful dinner. In some unfathomable way Mr Dearden had sensed her deep revulsion towards Cyril Ackroyd. Did he also sense her fear of Ackroyd's intentions? She didn't know. She only knew that that fear paralysed her with its intensity.

She was dimly aware that the maid had summoned them into the dining room and panic flooded through her. Miss Hawsley moved swiftly and took hold of Mr Dearden's arm before Bea had fully risen from her seat. She knew without a doubt that *her* intended dinner partner was to be Cyril Ackroyd. When he offered her the crook of his arm, she forced herself to look him straight in his eyes. 'Do not even touch me!' she hissed quietly, enunciating each word separately. She strode after the rest of the company with her spine held firmly erect.

The evening passed in a sense of unreality. Seated between Mr Hawsley and Mr Ackroyd, she felt trapped. Why were they doing this to her? Was Miss Hawsley so determined to capture

Mr Dearden that she had gone to the trouble of finding out the one other person who wished her evil? What other explanation was there? And, now that Ackroyd had discovered her whereabouts, she knew he didn't intend to slip quietly away again. Her only solution might be that she would have to disappear again – but how could she bear to leave? Where could she go?

'Have your eyes been troubling you, Miss Rossall?' Ackroyd asked in solicitous tones during a pause in the conversation. 'You used not to wear spectacles.'

Bea felt all eyes turn upon her. 'I am a governess, Mr Ackroyd,' she said coldly. 'I do a lot of close work.'

'Ah, so my friends the Hawsleys tell me. That is something else you used not to do.' He sighed loudly. 'And all so unnecessary, if only you hadn't spurned my generous offer. You brought the child with you, I hear. Was that wise, I wonder?'

Before Bea could speak, Mr Dearden took it upon himself to enter the conversation. 'Daisy's mother died in childbirth, leaving Daisy in Miss Rossall's keeping, as you undoubtedly know, Ackroyd. A commitment Miss Rossall takes very seriously – and she is to be greatly commended for doing so, especially as she does so in the face of much mean-spirited but unfounded gossip.'

Ackroyd's eyebrows rose. 'Miss Rossall's impetuous flight gave rise to a lot of gossip,' he agreed sanctimoniously. 'However, I am pleased to say, Miss Rossall, that I have taken steps to quell the gossip and your late father's parishioners are now willing to receive you, under my protection, back amongst them.' He swept his glance over his fellow diners. 'The Reverend Rossall was the living example of the Christian act of forgiveness. Such a pity that he was so broken at the end of his life.'

'My father died of ill-health and old age, Mr Ackroyd, not of a broken heart,' Bea snapped, angered by Ackroyd's insinuations. 'And I have no intention of returning to Salford in the foreseeable future.'

'It must be a little unsettling to know that your position will terminate when Mr Dearden's brother returns from his trip abroad,' Miss Hawsley said sweetly. 'What then, Miss Rossall? You may not find such an accommodating employer as Mr Dearden has proved to be. You might do well to hear what Mr Ackroyd has to offer you.'

'I think enough has been said on this matter,' Mr Dearden interposed. 'I am sure you will all agree that Miss Rossall's private life is not a matter for general comment over dinner.'

'Quite right, Dearden,' Mr Hawsley agreed. 'You do well to remind us, though our concern is out of genuine anxiety for her future, you understand. Do forgive us if the subject has embarrassed you in any way, Miss Rossall.'

Bea murmured a strangled acceptance. She wished she might flee the scene – but she lacked the self-possession to make a dignified exit. Nor did she make any further contribution to the conversation, knowing that her voice would betray her inner turmoil. She concentrated on pushing her food around her plate, longing for the meal to come to an end.

The half-hour whilst the gentlemen were enjoying their port seemed interminable. Neither of the Hawsley women made any attempt to speak pleasantly to her and the few remarks they did make were attempts to demoralize her further. Bea did the only thing she knew how – she silently prayed for strength to remain serene under such a barrage of hatred.

When the men returned Mr Dearden came straight to her side. Bea was grateful but was unable to respond to his attempts to put her at ease or draw her into the conversation. The whole evening had been a nightmare and she was thankful when Mr Dearden announced that it was time for them to leave. On the short journey home Mr Dearden kept up a light commentary, clearly not expecting to receive any response. All Bea longed for was the sanctity of her room, where she would be able at last to let the tears fall ... but even that haven was denied her when Mr Dearden opened the door of the sitting room and invited her inside.

'I know you must wish to retire but I feel we must talk for a short while. Do sit down.'

The fire had long since died away and Bea shivered as she sat down. Henry shrugged off his jacket and gently placed it around her shoulders. He squatted down in front of her, looking earnestly into her face. 'What do you suppose all that was about, Miss Rossall?' he asked. 'Why are the Hawsleys so eager to discredit you?'

Bea opened her mouth to reply but her breath caught in her throat. His head was just a bit lower than hers, which made it difficult to avoid meeting his glance. Her hands twisted round and round in her lap. Did he really not know why the Hawsleys were so against her? Why, even Winifred was aware of their motive! She made a poor effort at smiling. 'I fear they are very class-conscious. Your well-intentioned attempts to introduce me into society have outraged their sense of propriety.'

'But why produce Ackroyd? How did they know his being there would upset you? What did he do to you?' He took hold of her hands as he asked the last question, holding them still.

Bea swallowed hard. The memory of Ackroyd's assault still revolted her so much. She had temporarily thought she had left it behind – but she hadn't. It was so degrading. She still felt sullied by it. Dirty. She needed to wash, scrub herself each time she thought of it.

But Mr Dearden was awaiting an answer. 'Did he attack you in any way?' he asked gently, his eyes searching her face. 'Did her harm you?'

'He tried,' Bea whispered, 'but he didn't … hurt me. Not really. He … he pushed me back into a chair and fell on top of me.' She smiled tremulously. 'I rather think *I* hurt *him*. I drew up my knee and …' She couldn't say it but Mr Dearden grasped her meaning. He grinned appreciatively.

'Did you, by Jove! Good for you! So, what is he after now? He must realize you despise him.'

'He has lost face. He likes to control people, especially women.' Her voice was expressionless. She couldn't let herself feel any emotion if she were to be able to continue to speak. 'His late wife was afraid of him; she was a timid creature. She didn't stand a chance with him.' She shrugged, her mouth twisting wryly. 'He has had a succession of housekeepers since she died. He …' Her voice broke, became no more than a squeak. 'He … wanted me to take the place of the last one – but there were conditions attached. Conditions I wasn't prepared to accept.'

She glanced at his face. It was filled with revulsion. She'd known it would be. She was sullied, tainted, dishonoured. Any feelings he might have had for her were doomed. She shouldn't have told him. It had destroyed whatever hopes she might have had to win his love.

Henry was taken aback by the intensity of his fury. He clenched his fist. If Ackroyd were here, within arm's reach, he would floor him: he'd throttle him. He closed his eyes. He wanted to reach out to her but restrained himself. He must wait to see how things turned out. He stood up, closing his mind to the emotion he felt. 'Go to bed, Miss Rossall,' he said quietly. 'We will discuss this another time.'

Bea had seen the cold, closed expression on his face, just as she'd known it would be, and heard disgust in his voice. She stifled a cry, stopping it with the back of her hand. She ignored the hand he held towards her and rose to her feet unaided. His jacket fell unheeded to the floor as she fled from the room.

There was tension in the air over the next few days. Bea felt she couldn't face Mr Dearden over dinner and wrote him a terse note explaining that fact to him. *'I beg of you, do not seek to persuade me otherwise,'* she added, before signing her name.

She awaited his reply with some anxiety, wondering whether he would try to coax her to change her mind, maybe revealing to her that he had some understanding of the intolerable position Cyril Ackroyd had placed her in – but that was not to be. Instead, Mrs Kellett informed her that 'The master's dining with some of 'is colleagues for the next few evenings. Comin' to 'is senses, if you ask me!'

The only thing that lifted Bea's spirit was the girls' light-hearted expectation of the long-awaited fair that annually lined the path to the top of Rivington Pike with a variety of stalls and sideshows on Whit Sunday. Eliza Greenhalgh, invited to share the nursery tea one afternoon, regaled them with exciting tales of rolling pennies to win prizes and buying small toys, biscuits and bonbons.

'*Everybody* goes,' Eliza declared. 'Do say you will bring Winnie and Lily, Miss Rossall. And Daisy, too. Maybe Mr Dearden will come also? Mama and Papa will be taking me.'

Bea left it until Friday before approaching Mr Dearden with the request. When she responded to his peremptory 'Enter!' she realized that she hadn't chosen a good time. Mr Dearden was frowning at a letter he held in his hand. 'Yes?' he snapped.

Bea's confidence faltered. 'I'm sorry. You are busy. I'll come back some other time.' She began to retreat, drawing the door with her.

'No. Come back, Miss Rossall. I'm sorry. I am ...' He waved the letter impatiently and then laid it down. His voice softened. 'What was it you wished to speak to me about?'

Encouraged by the softening of his tone, Bea explained her request.

'Of course you may go. Take Gertie as well. I had meant to accompany you all but ...' He ran a hand distractedly through his hair. 'Now, it is impossible. I will be in Liverpool. Maybe for two or three days.' He paused, as if making up his mind whether or not to expand on his statement.

Bea was disappointed that he would be away but maybe it was for the best. 'I'm sorry. The girls were looking forward to your being with them. Never mind. Another time, perhaps.' She began to withdraw once more – but was again halted by his command.

'Don't go, Miss Rossall. I think I had better explain to you.' His voice seemed weary, defeated almost. 'Sit down ... please.' He waved his hand towards a chair and Bea obediently sat down, looking at him expectantly. He gestured at the letter. 'It's from my brother.'

'Oh? From Freddie?' Bea was instantly intrigued. 'Is he coming home?'

Mr Dearden smiled grimly. 'He is.'

Bea's expression lightened, although a shaft of pain hit her heart, too. Would his return herald the end of her employment here? But that was being selfish; she must think of the girls. 'Winifred and Lily will be pleased. When will it be? Shall I tell them or wait until nearer the time?'

He waved the letter again, his expression grim. 'He is in Liverpool at this moment, but he wants me to meet him before letting the girls know he is back in England. So, I depart to Liverpool first thing in the morning.'

Bea felt unsettled, aware that her days as Winifred's and Lily's governess might be numbered. Where would she go? She didn't know. She couldn't think straight, and it was pointless worrying about it yet. She concentrated on the girls, taking them and Eliza to fly their kites on Saturday afternoon after which they all had tea at the Greenhalghs' house. On Sunday morning they went to church. She noticed that Miss Hawsley was surprised to see them unescorted, and she felt a brief uncharitable surge of pleasure that Mr Dearden hadn't felt the need to inform her of his trip to Liverpool. She swiftly cast the thought aside, feeling relief that Cyril Ackroyd was not with the Hawsleys. She hoped he was back in Salford and that he would stay there!

After the service the girls slipped out of their pew to join Eliza, leaving Bea to walk down the aisle with Mr and Mrs Greenhalgh. She suspected that Miss Hawsley, a step or two in front of them, was listening to their conversation and she couldn't help feeling pleased that Mrs Greenhalgh was expressing her pleasure that the girls got on so well together.

'And where is Mr Dearden today?' Mrs Greenhalgh asked. 'I hope he isn't indisposed.'

'No. He had business to attend to in Liverpool. We hope that he will be back tomorrow.'

'But you are bringing his nieces to the Pike Fair this afternoon, aren't you, Miss Rossall? It is a very popular event with the local people. I am sure Eliza has been telling you all about it.'

'Yes, we are all coming. I am sure the girls will find each other there.'

Bea had been undecided whether or not to take Daisy, conscious of Mr Sharratt's request not to bring her too much to public notice in the company of his granddaughters. However, when Nanny Adams seemed to be a little under the weather she decided she must take the baby with them. By the time they set out quite a number of people were making their way to St George's Lane and up the rough track to the top of the Pike. The stalls and sideshows were assembled on the higher slopes along the track and there was a festive air among the crowds of people intent on having a good time. Winifred spotted Eliza Greenhalgh and was eager to join her.

'All right, but come back in about five minutes, then you can mind Daisy whilst I take Lily and Gertie to see the stalls,' Bea cautioned her.

'Do I have to? Can't you lift Daisy out of the pram and carry her?'

'No, she just fallen asleep and I'd rather she had a good nap. You know how cross she can be if she gets woken up too soon.'

'We could go on our own,' Lily offered hopefully.

Bea shook her head. 'No, there are too many people here and you might get lost amongst them. Winifred will come back soon, won't you, dear? I'll let you have a second turn after-wards.'

Winifred sighed heavily. 'All right, I suppose.' She scampered over to Eliza, leaving Lily in the company of Bea and Gertie.

Bea parked the pram and encouraged Lily and Gertie to play at jumping over the hummocks of grass for a while. A while later she caught sight of Winifred and Eliza. She waved to them, indicating that Lily and Gertie wanted to have their turn looking at the stalls. With a show of reluctance, Winifred said something to Eliza and returned to Bea.

'Isn't Eliza going to stay as well?' Bea asked.

'No, her mama said it's time they were going. They were here earlier than us. We've spent all our pennies, anyway.'

Bea gave Lily and Gertie some halfpennies and farthings and smiled at Winifred. 'Thank you, Winifred. We won't be long.'

None of them noticed a poorly clad woman hovering a few yards away. If they had, they might have wondered at the smoothness of her hands compared to the roughness of her clothes. She had watched in satisfaction when she saw the governess hold out her hands to Mr Dearden's younger niece and their grubby servant girl and let them pull her into the crowds around the stalls.

Now that fate had played into her hands, she felt a wave of nervousness wash over her, but she shrugged it away. She was doing Mr Dearden a service. He'd be grateful to her later, once he had had time to evaluate the outcome.

She signalled to the street urchin she had seen pick-pocketing one day and whom she had had the foresight to bring with her. 'Listen carefully,' she instructed him, 'and do exactly as I say.'

A few minutes later, Winifred saw a scruffy lad pointing to the ground at her feet. ''Ave yer dropped a penny, miss? If not, can I 'ave it?'

Winifred glanced down. Her eyes gleamed as she saw the penny and she quickly scooped it up. 'No, you can't! It must be mine.' A twinge of conscience made her hesitate. 'I tell you what. I'll buy some toffee with it and you can have a piece for being so honest.' There, that made her feel better. She glanced at the pram. Daisy was still fast asleep. It would only take a minute. Miss Rossall would never know. 'Come on, we'll have to be quick. I mustn't leave the baby for too long.'

Clutching the penny, she dived into the crowd, the young lad close on her heels. She feasted her eyes on the array of different kinds of toffees on the apron of the toffee stall. 'A penny mix, please.' She watched as the toffee-seller cracked pieces off a few different slabs of toffee and scooped them into a triangular twist of paper.

''Ere y'are, luv.'

Winifred selected a piece of toffee and grandly dropped it into the lad's grubby hand. 'There, that's for being so honest.' The lad quickly pushed it into his mouth and scampered away. Winifred popped a piece of caramel into her own mouth, savouring its sweetness – but she had better get back to Daisy before Miss Rossall realized she had left her unattended. She was almost back at the pram when she saw Miss Rossall returning with Lily and Gertie. She guiltily pushed the remains of the toffees into the pocket of her frock and skipped towards them.

'Is everything all right, Winifred?' Miss Rossall asked. She was smiling, so Winifred knew her hasty return hadn't been noticed. 'These two have spent all their pennies now, so you can go off again for a few minutes if you want to.'

'No, it's all right. I haven't any pennies left either.'

She glanced in the pram as she spoke. Her face froze. She turned her horrified face to Miss Rossall. 'Daisy's not there! Someone's taken her!'

Chapter 18

A MAN WHOM Bea didn't know took charge of the situation and sent someone running off to the local police station. The girls were hysterical, especially Winifred, and Bea was glad when she eventually got them home. She felt hysterical herself but tried to subdue her fears.

'It's my fault!' Winifred kept crying. 'I shouldn't have left her! I was only away a minute or two. I'm sorry! I'm sorry! I shouldn't have gone.'

Although Bea knew it was true as far as it went, she blamed herself for putting a ten-year-old in charge of Daisy. She wrapped her arms around Winifred and held her close. 'No, no. The main fault is mine,' she tried to reassure her.

That was certainly Mrs Kellett's opinion. 'Huh! Can't even mind your own child!' she sneered. 'Mr Dearden'll never leave you in charge of his nieces after this.'

Bea found that less of a concern than getting Daisy back. Who could have taken her? Why? Was it someone who had recently miscarried a baby and had taken her on impulse to try to ease her own hurt? That was possible. If so, would her family or neighbours persuade her to return Daisy? She preferred that possibility to others that lurked on the fringes of her mind. She wished Mr Dearden were home. He would have taken charge and pushed the investigations forward. The constable had been kind enough but she felt that he blamed her carelessness. Maybe he was right? If only she could turn back the clock!

In the solace of her room she went over the facts that the police constable had managed to extract from Winifred. A ragged urchin had pointed out a penny at Winifred's feet. Why would an urchin do that? Wouldn't he just scoop up the coin and run? Where had the coin come from? Winifred said she had spent all her pennies. Had she herself dropped it when giving pennies to Lily and Gertie? No, she hadn't given them pennies. She had given them halfpennies and farthings.

That thought stilled her. It seemed a great coincidence that a penny should suddenly appear at Winifred's feet just when someone who wanted to steal a baby was in the vicinity. Had someone been watching them? Waiting for such an opportunity? Who could possibly have anything to gain by taking Daisy away?

A sudden chill seized her heart. There were two people who wished her harm. Cyril Ackroyd was certainly ruthless enough – and he wouldn't care what happened to Daisy afterwards. Did Miss Hawsley hate her enough to risk such an undertaking?

She spent a restless, almost sleepless, night and rose early. She felt lost without Daisy to see to. She washed and dressed, her heart leaden within her. She was about to go to the nursery, when she heard the sound of the front gate clanging shut. Was it someone with news of Daisy's safe return? She rushed to the window. The gate was still quivering on its hinges but she couldn't see anyone. She spun around and hurried down the stairs. A small folded paper lay on the doormat. She snatched it up and undid the fold with trembling fingers. It read:

I have something of yours which you might care to have returned. Come alone to the rear of Bob's Smithy at 10 o'clock this morning to discuss the matter. If you do not come alone your 'possession' will be disposed of by other means.

Bea sank on to the chair by the side table. She stared at the note in her hand. Who had written it? Ackroyd? Miss Hawsley? Did it matter? The end would be the same – she would have to leave Endmoor House. She dropped her head into her hands. She had no choice.

However, there was something she could do. She returned to her room and found a piece of paper. She wrote:

Mr Dearden, after receiving the enclosed note, I have gone to meet its author, whom I suspect to be either Cyril Ackroyd or a 'certain lady' of your acquaintance. I may be unable to return and I am sorry if my leaving causes any inconvenience to you. You will have learned that Daisy was stolen from her perambulator yesterday. I MUST do all I can to get her back. Thank you for all you have done for me. I very much appreciate it. I hope your brother now takes good care of his daughters. Please do not let Winifred continue to blame herself for Daisy's abduction. The fault was mine for not being aware that such an event might take place.
Beatrice Rossall.

It was a subdued quartet who met in the nursery for breakfast. Bea would have liked to tell Nanny Adams what she was about to do, but not in front of the girls. They had been in tears throughout breakfast and Bea knew that her leaving would cause more but she couldn't see any other way to get Daisy back. At least Winifred and Lily had a father, an uncle and a devoted nanny, whereas she and Daisy only had each other.

She asked Nanny Adams if she would take care of the girls during the morning, letting Nanny assume she was going to the police station. She then dressed in the clothes she had worn on her arrival, and packed her other frock and few personal possessions into her shabby portmanteau, leaving the gowns Nanny Adams had helped her to alter hanging in the wardrobe. Daisy's things were in the nursery; she would have to leave those. If all went well she would be able to replace them.

She paused in the doorway of her room and looked around sadly. She had been happy here; far happier than she had dared hope. Now it was over. She turned away and quietly slipped down the stairway and out through the front door, closing it silently behind her.

A carriage stood behind Bob's smithy, blinds drawn at its windows. A coachman sat ready on its high seat and a young lad stood at the horses' heads, holding the bridles. At her approach he ran forward, opened the carriage door and let down the step. Bea halted, reluctant to enter the carriage before she knew who was inside.

'Get into the carriage, Miss Rossall. You are wasting time,' Cyril Ackroyd voice spoke.

Bea took a step back. She couldn't help it. Fear rose in her throat. 'Where's Daisy? You said you would give her back to me. I won't come without Daisy.'

'The child is safe. You will be reunited at our destination. However, she is not the only one you need to consider. I also have in my keeping your former housekeeper. She refuses to co-operate in fulfilling the role of housekeeper that I insist upon. If you do not come with me, I will beat her into submission – and make sure your child is lost to you permanently.'

Bea's mind spun around. What was he talking about? 'Mrs Hurst? You are lying. Mrs Hurst went to live with her sister. She would never work for you.'

'You underestimate what a desperate person will do when faced with the prospect of no home and no food, Miss Rossall. Mrs Hurst's sister died before she left Salford. Without references, she was unable to get employment and was faced with the workhouse – or working for me. She chose the latter.'

'You stopped people from employing her,' Bea accused him. 'You are an evil man.'

He laughed harshly. 'I care not what people think of me, Miss Rossall. However, we waste time. You alone have the means of determining the future of the two people you are most concerned about and my patience is wearing thin. Get into this carriage or know for ever that it was you who consigned those two people to a life of misery.'

Bea hesitated. Could she trust him? The answer was 'no' – but she had no other choice.

'Put up the step, boy, and close the door,' Ackroyd commanded.

The lad bent down to lift the step. She had to decide right now. 'Wait! All right, I'll come with you – but I will not agree to your plans until I have seen Daisy and made sure Mrs Hurst is released!'

Silence greeted her statement. Bea knew her bargaining power was almost non-existent. Maybe, when she and Mrs Hurst were together, they would be able to withstand Ackroyd better than when alone. With a desperate silent plea for the Lord to be with her, Bea clambered into the carriage. As soon as the door was closed the carriage lurched forward.

She was thankful that Ackroyd didn't seem to expect any conversation and Bea had no wish to speak to him, so the journey was conducted in silence. She was incensed when Ackroyd gripped her arm tightly whilst hurrying her through the ticket barrier and on to the platform.

'You have no need to hold on me,' she said coldly. 'You have made sure of my acquiescence by the underhand tactics you have used.'

'I'll be holding you a lot more closely than this before the day it out,' he sneered, 'so you had better get used to it.'

Bea shuddered. Not if she could help it, he wouldn't!

It felt strange to be back in the familiar streets of Salford. It was mid-afternoon and she had hoped she might see someone she knew; someone who might be able to give assistance to her once she had Daisy safely in her arms and had ensured Mrs Hurst's release, but Ackroyd hustled her from the hired carriage and into his house before she could glance up or down the street.

Determined not to be cowed by Ackroyd, Bea instantly demanded to be given Daisy.

'You'll see her when it pleases me,' Ackroyd snapped. 'And that won't be until *you* have pleased me!'

'Then we are at stalemate,' Bea declared.

'You may like to think so – but you are mistaken. You won't get the better of me again, Miss Rossall. I am looking forward to making you pay for that little episode – and be assured of this, I *will* bed you before this day is over. However, we will have some refreshments first. You are probably anxious to meet my new housekeeper. I will go and let her out of her room.'

'You locked her in?'

'Only since Saturday afternoon. No doubt she will be more inclined to do as she is told.'

'You are despicable!'

'So people tell me. The ones who don't know how to please me. I shall enjoy teaching *you* how to please me, Miss Rossall. You can start now by accompanying me upstairs.'

'No!'

'Less of the histrionics, Miss Rossall. This excursion upstairs is to let Mrs Hurst see the success of my plan. She will, no doubt, be very glad to see you.'

He gripped her arm again and marched her up the stairs. Bea wished she could resist but she would rather Mrs Hurst were free before she made her attempt to escape – and she still hadn't seen Daisy. Where was she? Was she sleeping? Had Ackroyd engaged a nursemaid for her?

Ackroyd halted outside a door and took a bunch of keys from his pocket. He fitted one into the lock and opened the door. An unpleasant smell wafted out of the room, causing Ackroyd to curl his lips in disdain. He pushed Bea in front of him and she stumbled into the room.

Her former housekeeper was crouched upon her bed, looking a sorry sight. Her hair and clothes were dishevelled, her face ravaged with fear and worry. She struggled to sit up and, at the sight of Bea, she burst into tears. 'Oh, Miss Bea, why did you come? You should've just left me. I didn't want you to come here.'

'Such ingratitude,' Ackroyd sneered. 'And there I was thinking how delighted you would be.'

Bea rushed forward. 'Mrs Hurst, you poor thing! I'm so sorry to see you like this.' She turned round on Ackroyd. 'This is inhuman. You are no gentleman, sir!'

'Yes, yes. We've had all that before. Save your pity for yourself.'

Bea looked at him scornfully. 'How dare you treat a woman so cruelly? You must let me air this room and make Mrs Hurst more comfortable before we go any further.' She thought quickly, and then added, 'After that, I will make a meal for us all. I presume you have food in the house?'

'Very well – but no talking together! I will be listening. And remember the other matter. Any tricks and that will be the end of that!'

Bea believed him. He was capable of anything. She set to with a will to make Mrs Hurst more comfortable. She found the bathroom and emptied the chamber pot; she took a bowl of water and washed Mrs Hurst's face and hands; and brushed her hair. When she had done all she could, she turned back to Ackroyd, keeping her face impassive. 'I'll go to the kitchen now and see what there is to make into a meal.'

Ackroyd stood back and let her pass, hopefully now assured that she wouldn't leave Mrs Hurst to his mercy. Bea's main concern was to locate Daisy and work out a plan how to get all three of them away from this house. She hoped a good meal would subdue all other appetites Cyril Ackroyd might have.

One item in the store cupboard brought a gleam to her eyes. It was a large brown bottle labelled 'laxative'. Now, a good dose of that, concealed in some food or other, might incapacitate their captor.

When Mr Dearden arrived home just before noon the house was unnaturally quiet, almost as it used to be before his nieces came to live with him. Somehow, it no longer seemed as appealing as it used to do. Maybe that was as well, considering the news he had to impart – but not until he had discussed its implications with Miss Rossall.

But, before that, he had better wash away the smuts of smoke after the train journey from Liverpool. His right-hand knuckles were sore, too. He winced as he lightly touched them.

How out of character had that been, flooring his own brother? He had no regrets though. Freddie deserved it. Not that it would make any difference in the long run – but it had made him feel satisfied to see Freddie's look of surprise as he fell backwards.

His toilet seen to, he strode along the corridor to the schoolroom at the far end to let Miss Rossall and his nieces know he was home again – but it was empty. Had Miss Rossall taken her pupils on another discovery trip around the town? Was that why the house was so quiet? Nanny Adams would know.

He went to the nursery and was surprised to see his nieces encased in Nanny Adams's arms, the three of them snuggled together on the sofa. As their faces turned towards him, he could see at once that they were all distressed. His heart leaped in alarm. 'Where is Miss Rossall? And Daisy? Is one of them ill?'

'Oh, Uncle Henry!' Winifred cried out, running to him and flinging herself against him, hugging his middle. 'You're back! You'll know what to do! You'll bring them back, won't you?'

'Hey! Hey! What's the matter? Bring who back?' His mind began to reach its own answer. His voice sharpened. 'What's happened? Where's Miss Rossall?'

'We don't know!' Winifred wailed. 'She's gone. She didn't come back!'

'Didn't come back from where?' He looked over her head at Nanny Adams.

Her expression did nothing to reassure him. 'Oh, Mr Dearden,' she wailed. 'Daisy was took and Miss Rossall went to the police station this morning but she's not come back. We didn't know what to do!'

Henry disengaged himself from Winifred's hold and guided her back to the sofa. He sat her down again, then crouched in front of them. 'Now take a deep breath, Nanny, and then start again at the beginning.'

The whole tale came out in a disjointed fashion but he quickly got the hang of it. 'Right! I will go to the police station immediately and find out what happened.'

He hurried into town as quickly as was decently possible, telling himself that it was bound to be some sort of misunderstanding that he would be able to sort out easily. His anxiety returned when he discovered that Miss Rossall had not spoken to the police that day, neither had any information come to light regarding Daisy's disappearance.

'It's sometimes the mother, in cases like this,' the duty sergeant suggested. 'We'll need to question her further.'

'Don't be ridiculous!' Henry snapped. 'She adores that baby. I need to find her.'

'We're doing all we can, sir. Like I said, we need to question Miss Rossall again. Maybe if I send someone round now?'

'Aren't you listening, man? I've just told you. She isn't here. She's missing, too.'

'Ah!'

At the sergeant's satisfied sigh, Henry turned on his heels and strode back to his home, trying to make sense of what he had been told. Had Miss Rossall left voluntarily, with no intention of going to the police station? He ran back upstairs and burst into Miss Rossall's room. Everything looked tidy – too tidy! He opened the wardrobe door and saw her gowns hanging there. That was a good sign, but something made him stop. Where were her coat and the large bag that she had brought her possessions in? He pulled open a few drawers. They were empty. His spirits sank. She had gone.

But where? Contrary to the police sergeant's opinion, she *wasn't* responsible for Daisy's disappearance. Besides, he had

Winifred's confession as to what had happened. No, if Miss Rossall had gone, it was because she had some idea where Daisy might be. Had she confided in his housekeeper? Would that be a natural thing for a woman to do?

He rushed down to the kitchen. 'Mrs Kellett!' he roared as he entered, his anxiety having deprived him of all his usual politeness. 'What do you know of all this? Surely someone knows where Miss Rossall has gone? Didn't she tell you where she was going?'

Mrs Kellett glared indignantly at him, her face flushed an ugly red. 'How should I know where she is? She didn't take *me* into 'er confidences. Thought 'erself above the likes of us, she did. You're well rid of 'er, if you ask me. I told you you'd made a mistake takin' 'er on.'

'Thank you, Mrs Kellett. When I want such advice, I will ask for it. Until then, keep such thoughts to yourself!' He ignored Mrs Kellett's indignant 'Well!' and turned to where Gertie was skulking in a corner of the kitchen looking as though she had been crying for the past twenty-four hours. 'What about you, Gertie? You went to the Pike Fair with Miss Rossall and my nieces, didn't you? Did you notice anything untoward? Come now, don't be afraid,' he added in gentler tones, seeing Gertie cast anxious glances at Mrs Kellett. 'I'm not angry with you – nor with Mrs Kellett. I'm sorry to be shouting. It's because I am so anxious about Miss Rossall and Daisy.'

He crouched before her, certain that she wanted to tell him something. He wasn't mistaken.

With anxious looks cast towards Mrs Kellett, Gertie muttered, 'There was a letter, sir. It was in 'er room, on 'er dressin' table. I gived it to Mrs Kellett but she threw it away.'

Henry straightened up. Mrs Kellett's face gave her away, even though she indignantly denied it. 'She's lyin'! I never 'eard such nonsense! You just wait, you little liar! I'll wallop you for saying such things and then you can pack up an' go!'

Gertie shrank away from her and darted behind Henry in an effort to run out of the kitchen, but Henry stopped her, his hand on her shoulder. 'Go up to the nursery, Gertie. Tell Nanny Adams I want her to look after you until I come. Go on. No one will harm you.'

Once she had gone, he faced Mrs Kellett. He knew she had resented Miss Rossall from the start but hadn't thought she would actually act against her. It was now obvious that she had.

'Where is the letter, Mrs Kellett?' He hoped she hadn't destroyed it. 'Was it addressed to me?' When there was no response, he added, 'I have already spoken to the police sergeant at the station. He is sending a constable here to ask further questions of us all. I would advise you to tell me what you have done with the letter before he gets here. I may be able to help to lessen the penalty for tampering with evidence.' He was stretching the truth but it was all he could think of.

Mrs Kellett's indignation crumpled. 'It didn't 'ave no name on it. 'Ow was I to know who it was for?' she stammered. 'I threw it in the bin.'

'Then you had better retrieve it, Mrs Kellett.'

After a moment's hesitation, Mrs Kellett crossed over to the waste bin and rummaged amongst its variety of contents, eventually withdrawing the crumpled letter. 'Yer'll be too late. She's gone with 'im. Your Miss Hawsley told me she was engaged to marry 'im. I wouldn't be surprised if the babby turns out to be 'is! Like I said, I knew she wasn't to be trusted.'

Henry was barely listening. He had smoothed out the two

letters and was reading them. Miss Rossall hadn't named the woman she suspected, but Henry knew whom she thought it was. The same one whom Mrs Kellett had just mentioned.

Chapter 19

HENRY WAS SO full of anxiety over Miss Rossall's and Daisy's safety that he didn't beat about the bush when he arrived at the Hawsleys' house. His curt demand to speak to Miss Hawsley was met with raised eyebrows, followed by a calculating gleam in Mrs Hawsley's eyes.

'Ah! Was your trip to Liverpool successful, Mr Dearden? It was for something special, perhaps?' She tapped his arm coyly. 'I think I understand the urgency in your request to speak to Caroline. If you will step into the drawing-room, I will call her down.'

Henry very much doubted she knew the reason behind his urgency, not unless Miss Rossall's disappearance had been brought about by a family conspiracy, which seemed a little unlikely. It was more probably the act of a spiteful woman.

Miss Hawsley entered the room, obviously primed by her mother's misconception. 'Mr Dearden! This is an honour – and quite unexpected.' She seated herself on an upright chair, fluttered her eyelashes and smiled up at him in what might have been an attempt at a guileless expression. To Henry it seemed more like the smile on a fox's face as it entered the hen-coop.

'You are still standing, Mr Dearden. Aren't you going to kn ... er ... sit down?'

'No, thank you, Miss Hawsley. What I have to say will not

take long.' His voice was sharp and he noted Miss Hawsley's surprise with some satisfaction. 'I want to know the whereabouts of Daisy Brindle, and Ackroyd's address in Salford.'

Miss Hawsley's hand fluttered at her throat. 'B...but how do you expect me to know that? He ... he is a business acquaintance of my father. You must ask him.'

'Oh, I will, if I get no satisfaction from you. But somehow I can't see your father's hand behind all this, whereas it sits quite easily upon you. How did you find out about Ackroyd? Having met him, I can understand Miss Rossall's loathing of him, yet you have conspired to lure her into his clutches – using an innocent babe to do so. You are as despicable as he is!'

'Oh!' Miss Hawsley stared at him in horrified realization that her scheme had backfired on her. The thought filled her with fury and she rallied her spirit. 'Mr Ackroyd was distraught by Miss Rossall's desertion of him, Mr Dearden. He was delighted to learn of her whereabouts. I knew at once that he was very much in love with her. I merely engineered their reunion – instead of standing by and allowing her to ensnare a man above her station.'

Henry raised his eyebrows. 'It wasn't love I saw in his eyes, Miss Hawsley. I saw something I wouldn't want to inflict on any young lady, but you saw fit to deliver Miss Rossall into his hands, knowing how desperate she would be to get Daisy back. Where is Daisy, Miss Hawsley? I am sure she won't be at Ackroyd's home in Salford when Miss Rossall arrives to claim her.'

Miss Hawsley fluttered her hand. 'Poof! You are making a fuss over nothing, Mr Dearden! Of what account is Miss Rossall's bastard child to a gentleman of your standing? You should be grateful to me, not standing there berating me in this unseemly manner! If I hadn't removed her from your patronage, tongues would have been busy wagging before much longer!'

Henry felt anger surge through him. How had he ever managed to overlook Miss Hawsley's spiteful ways? 'Daisy is not Miss Rossall's bastard child, Miss Hawsley. She is my brother's child – my niece. So I will ask you once more – before I am forced to hand the enquiry over to the constabulary, who, by the way, are already involved in investigating Daisy's abduction – what is Ackroyd's address and what have you done with Daisy?'

Miss Hawsley stared at him, her hand partly covering her open mouth. 'She is y ... your ... niece?' she echoed. Her eyes suddenly gleamed and her mouth set in a grim line of satisfaction. 'So, I was right. Miss Rossall—'

'No,' Henry interrupted, refusing to hear any further slur upon Miss Rossall's character from this woman. 'Miss Rossall's involvement is only by way of her Christian charity in caring for an abandoned orphan – and if I hear of any rumours circulating about either Miss Rossall or my brother, I will know from whom they have originated and, have no doubt, Miss Hawsley, I *will* inform the police of your involvement. So, Ackroyd's address? This instant!'

Miss Hawsley knew defeat when she saw it and, with sullen grace, she told him Ackroyd's address in Salford.

'And Daisy? What have you done with her?'

'She's quite safe. I ... gave her to a friend, who had agreed to ... to find a home for her.'

'Then it is to be hoped that your "friend" is able to return her without delay. I will allow you twenty-four hours, and have no doubt, Miss Hawsley, I will hold you responsible for any ill-treatment she may have suffered since her abduction.'

Having obtained the information he needed, Henry left

immediately, leaving Miss Hawsley to explain his purpose and abrupt departure to her mother in whatever way she chose.

The thought of what might be happening to Miss Rossall urged him on. He stopped at his house only long enough to tell Nanny Adams that the search for Daisy would soon be over and that he now knew Miss Rossall's intended destination. He just hoped he would get there in time to prevent whatever unpleasantness Ackroyd had planned for her.

Why had it taken him so long to realize how precious Miss Rossall had become to him? He had been ready to admit that he admired her and enjoyed the pleasure of her company – but he now knew it was more than that. He wanted more than her company – he wanted her as his wife. It had been bad enough to hear his brother trying to deny any involvement; trying to make out that she was trying to blackmail him for monetary recompense – but this was much worse. He couldn't bear the thought of that vile Ackroyd destroying her innocence. He all but ran to the railway station. He knew he was taking a risk by not informing the police of his discoveries but, in spite of Miss Hawsley's wicked intentions, he felt he must give her the opportunity to redeem her actions insofar as she was able.

Never had rail travel seemed so slow. With two connections to make, it was late afternoon when he arrived in Salford. There he hailed a cab and gave directions to the driver, stopping first at a local police station, where he recounted as much of the tale as he thought necessary.

The desk sergeant listened with interest. He had heard tales of the so-called 'gentleman' involved in this unsavoury abduction and felt inclined to believe them. 'We're a bit short on spare constables today, sir, what with the Whitsuntide Walks through the city centre. But I know a couple of heavyweight boxers who are handy to have around in times of trouble. We'll be right behind you!'

Henry hurried outside the waiting cab.

Bea had found a large piece of lean beefsteak, which she made into a savoury stew. Desperate to delay the impending confrontation with Ackroyd, she took her time as she peeled and prepared the vegetables, hoping her plan to incapacitate Ackroyd would work swiftly. She now realized that she wouldn't find Daisy here in this house. Daisy was probably still in Horwich – how stupid she had been to believe Ackroyd! She had rushed away without thinking it through! She felt desperate with worry, but Mrs Hurst also needed her help and she couldn't just abandon her.

When the meal was ready to be served she made up a plate for Mrs Hurst and took it to Ackroyd's small sitting room. She forced herself to speak pleasantly. 'Dinner is ready, Mr Ackroyd. May I take this plate up to Mrs Hurst before we eat? She must be very hungry, having had very little to eat since Saturday.'

'I'll tek it. I don't want you plotting with 'er.' He took the tray from her hands. 'You can tek ours into the dining room. You know where it is.' He leered at her. 'The smell o' this is whettin' me appetite – an' not just for the food! So get on with it!'

Back in the kitchen, Bea ladled out a small portion of the stew for herself. She paused with the bottle of laxative syrup in her hand. How much would she need to incapacitate Ackroyd? She removed the stopper, poured a liberal amount into the remainder of the stew and stirred it in. She touched the edge of the spoon with the tip of her tongue. Mmm, a slight flavour of figs. Nice!

Bea had no appetite for food, but felt a surge of satisfaction as Ackroyd shovelled the stew into his mouth. The dinner progressed in near silence, except when his hand slid under the table and he gripped hold of her knee.

'Please don't do that,' she objected.

'I'll do as I damn well please!' he returned, smiling unpleasantly. 'You're 'ere now. You'll do as I say.'

Not without a fight, she wouldn't! However, Bea realized that she needed to keep him talking to give the laxative time to work. 'I am prepared to … consider … your request, if you will release Mrs Hurst – and once I know Daisy is safe.'

Ackroyd was unperturbed by her declaration. 'You'll do more than consider it – and I make the decisions round 'ere, not you. Remember that!'

He continued to eat his meal and Bea found herself watching every forkful that went into his mouth. She did little more than push her own food around her plate, her appetite quite diminished. Keep him talking, she bade herself. 'You will find that I am not the type of person who is easily pushed around, Mr Ackroyd. How do you intend to keep me here? Locked in a room, as you have locked in Mrs Hurst? Sooner or later, someone will realize I am a prisoner in the house. How will you explain that? I will not keep silent about what you are doing. Neither will Mrs Hurst.'

A flicker of uncertainty flashed in his eyes but he dismissed it instantly. 'Yer'll be too shamed to tell anyone – and don't forget the babby. If yer want to see 'er agen, yer'll do as I say – and that dried-up old prune upstairs will, too, if she knows what's good fer 'er.'

Bea flinched at his coarseness but avoided looking at him. How long would it take the laxative to work? She fought to suppress her fears. 'I don't believe you have Daisy,' she said boldly. 'I would know if she were here. And Mrs Hurst has already told me to leave her. I think you will find you have taken on more than you can handle!'

Ackroyd continued to clear his plate. The sight sickened her. She needed to get away from him. She rose from her chair and pushed it back a little. 'I'll go back to the kitchen and bring in the apple charlotte. It should be ready by now.'

Ackroyd's hand clamped on to her arm. 'Sit down, Miss Rossall. You're going nowhere. We'll 'ave the puddin' later – after I've worked up my appetite a bit.'

Bea sat down again, curling her fingers around the handle of her knife. She'd use it, if she had to. She would! Ackroyd picked up his napkin with his other hand and wiped his lips; then, still clasping her arm, he stood, pushing his chair aside. 'Enough o' talkin'! We'll go upstairs right now.'

'No.' He would have to drag her – and she would fight him all the way!

His hand moved so fast, the stinging slap that knocked her sideways from her chair took Bea completely by surprise.

'Ouch!'

Her head hit the edge of the table as she fell, dislodging her spectacles and making stars dance before her eyes. Temporarily disorientated, she lay in a crumpled heap, her mind befuddled.

Ackroyd dropped down on top of her. 'Now we'll see what you're made of,' he grunted, ripping open her bodice. Her scream was cut off abruptly as he clamped his mouth over hers, thrusting his tongue into her mouth.

Filled with revulsion, Bea struggled desperately as his left hand pulled up her skirt. She tried to jerk her lower body away from his groping hand but his weight prevented her. Her hand was pinned at her side. He lifted his head to gloat over her feeble efforts and Bea seized the opportunity to scream as loudly as she could – though who was to hear her, she couldn't imagine.

Henry jumped out of the cab. The house looked cold and uninviting. It was a solid, square building, double-fronted with a window on either side of the front door. The curtains weren't closed and, at first, Henry wondered whether he had been mistaken in thinking Ackroyd would bring Miss Rossall to his home. He walked uncertainly up the path, glancing towards the left-hand window. The room seemed empty. Then he heard a scream. He darted to the window. Inside the room, he saw a black-coated male figure pinning down a female who was struggling to be free of him. He couldn't see her face but he had no doubt as to who she was.

Anger surged through him. He ran to the door, yelling to the cab-driver, 'Come with me!' as he ferociously kicked open the door and hurtled down the short entrance hall. Once in the room, he strode the few paces to the struggling pair, grabbed hold of the man by the collar of his coat and hauled him upright. Without pausing, he aimed a blow at the man's head. Ackroyd's head snapped back, his eyes wide with surprise.

Henry followed him down, his well-aimed fists finding their mark with each blow. Ackroyd, taken unawares and over-whelmed by the young man's rage, could do nothing to protect himself.

Henry became aware of booted feet around him and a gruff voice saying, 'We'll take over now, sir,' and he looked up to see the police sergeant and two other men towering over them. He glanced down at Ackroyd. He looked a sorry sight. There would be no further resistance from him. Henry prised himself off the man and staggered to his feet.

The cab driver had assisted Miss Rossall to her feet and had led her to a chair. She was clutching the torn edges of her bodice together with one hand, her face aflame with embarrassment. In her other hand she held her crushed spectacles. Henry swiftly moved to her side and leaned over her, the backs of his fingers lightly brushing against her cheek. 'Are you all right, my dear? He hasn't … harmed you?' His voice was tender, his eyes concerned.

Bea shook her head, meeting his eyes for a brief moment before casting them down again. She no longer cared about the spectacles. It had been a foolish notion, anyway. She caught sight of his bruised and bleeding knuckles. 'You're hurt.'

Henry tried to flex his fingers and winced. 'Yes, but I'll mend.' He turned to cast a loathing look at Ackroyd. 'It was worth it.'

'Arrest that man, Sergeant!' Ackroyd blustered through swollen lips. 'You've caught him in the act of inflicting grievous bodily assault! He burst in here and attacked my dinner companion and then turned on me when I tried to defend her. Isn't that so, Miss Rossall?'

Bea regarded him with disgust. 'No, it is not!' she contradicted him. 'You brought me here under false pretences and then assaulted me, attempting to … to …' She couldn't put it into words. She turned to the police sergeant. 'You will find another lady locked in a room upstairs. She is my former housekeeper. I must go to her at once.'

The sergeant nodded towards the two men who had accompanied him. 'Go upstairs with Miss Rossall and 'elp 'er 'ousekeeper down the stairs. Fetch everythin' yer might need, miss. Yer won't be wanting to come back 'ere.'

Ackroyd tried to shake off the hands that had hauled him to his feet. 'This is preposterous! I am a respectable mill-owner, Sergeant. You'll surely not take the word of a woman of loose morals over mine. She's trying to blacken my—' Ackroyd suddenly grasped hold of his lower abdomen, his face paling dramatically. 'I feel ill,' he gasped. 'I'm going to—'

'Stop play-acting!' Henry snapped. 'You'll get no sympathy from us.'

'I think he might need to get to a lavatory,' Bea said smugly. 'I laced his stew with laxative.'

Ackroyd tried to lunge at her but was restrained. 'You...! You'll pay for this! I'll mek sure of it. Urgh!' He groaned as another griping pain sliced through his abdomen.

'Tek 'im down the yard,' the sergeant commanded the two men holding Ackroyd, as an unpleasant smell began to fill the room. 'Mek sure 'e plays no tricks on you. Then we'll sort every-thin' out at the station. I'll be wanting statements from the lot of you.'

It was well into the evening by the time the sergeant was satis-fied with their statements and Henry felt that it would be too much to expect Mrs Hurst to travel to Horwich that day. Although Bea was anxious about Daisy's whereabouts, she agreed to spend the night in a hotel recommended by the helpful cab-driver.

Aware of her torn loyalties, Henry took hold of both her hands. 'Miss Hawsley knows where Daisy is. I gave her twenty-four hours to bring her back to you. She should be there when we return tomorrow.'

Bea felt faint with relief and feared she was about to fall. She was thankful that Mr Dearden led her to sit on a sofa. He sat down beside her, still holding her hands. 'Before we return home, Miss Russall, I must speak of what took place in Liverpool.'

Bea's heart lurched. Did his brother want to take Winifred and Lily away immediately? And what about Daisy? Would he take her, also? She tried to hide her anxiety but her voice belied that resolve. 'I hope we get Daisy back whilst your brother is here. I'm sure he'll love her as much as I do. Is he at your house?'

Henry's face changed. He gripped her hands even more tightly but all sign of tenderness had gone from his face. 'No, he isn't. He's not coming – not yet, anyway!'

Bea was bewildered. 'Not coming? Surely he wants to see Winifred and Lily? Isn't that why he has come home?'

Henry looked grim. 'He has come home to tell me of his new marriage – to the daughter of a New York banker. They are, at present, on an extensive tour of Europe and will be leaving Liverpool tomorrow on their way to the Continent.' He released her hands as he flexed his right fist, seeming to relish in the cuts and bruises there, as he laughed harshly. 'I'm afraid I hit him.'

Bea dropped her gaze to his sore knuckles. 'I expect he deserved it. He wouldn't accept that Daisy is his child, would he?'

'No, he wouldn't. He even tried to make out that she is mine. Not that I—'

'It's all right,' Bea sighed. 'I more or less expected it.' It left her no worse off than before, and her job as Winifred and Lily's governess would be secure for a while longer.

Suddenly, she felt very tired. The day's events had taken a greater toll than she had thought. She smiled wanly as she touched Mr Dearden's arm. 'Thank you for coming so swiftly to rescue me. I appreciate it more than I can say. But I must retire now. Will we be able to set off to return to Horwich as early as possible? I am anxious to see Daisy again.'

Henry agreed, wondering whether Miss Rossall's interruption of what he had been about to say had been a good thing –

or not. It might be better said when Daisy was actually back in their midst.

They were a subdued trio on the return journey to Horwich. Mrs Hurst was full of gratitude that she was returning with them but was too shocked and upset by the recent months of harsh employment by Mr Ackroyd to be able to do much more than to express her thanks repeatedly.

Bea was content to gaze at the green fields they passed through and was almost overcome by the sense of 'coming home' when she saw Rivington Pike standing out proudly on the hillside. All she wanted was to be back in that stone house at the foot of the moors – with Daisy in her arms. *Please let Daisy be there*! she prayed silently.

Henry shared her anxiety – and wondered how Miss Rossall would react towards the proposal he intended to make. Would she agree? Or would she refuse to consider it?

Bea was barely aware of arriving in Horwich, nor of being handed up into a carriage at the station. Her anxiety grew the nearer they came to Endmoor House. As she hurried up the garden path the door was flung open and Winifred stood in the doorway with Daisy in her arms. Just behind her, Nanny Adams, Lily and Gertie crowded forward to greet their return.

'Daisy's here, Miss Rossall!' Winifred cried. 'She's here!'

Bea ran the last few steps and received Daisy into her outstretched arms, instantly smothering her with kisses, delighting in Daisy's coos and happy babblings. 'It doesn't matter that you haven't got a papa, Daisy,' she murmured without thought, unaware that tears of joy were running down her face. 'All that matters is that you're safe!'

A slight cough beside her made her look towards Mr Dearden. He seemed strangely ill at ease for some reason – but before Bea had had time to try to work out why, he said hesitantly, 'It mightn't be the proper time to say this – but I am going to do so, anyway.' He gave another cough to clear his throat. 'I'd like to become Daisy's father – if you will allow me, Miss Rossall?'

Bea stared at him. 'You? But you aren't married. What will people say?'

'I don't care what people will say. With you at my side, we will outface them all together! What do you say?'

'M … me? At your side?'

Henry laughed at himself. 'I'm sorry. I seem to have missed out the most important question. Will you marry me, Miss Rossall? I intended to ask you last night but I knew you were tired. I have been slowly falling in love with you – and, when you weren't here when I returned home from Liverpool, I knew I didn't want to live without you. So, what do say, Miss Rossall? Can you learn to love me and become aunt instead of governess to my two rascally nieces?'

Bea was aware that Winifred was eying her anxiously – but the light in her eyes expressed the girl's hope that she would say 'yes', and Lily was already excitedly jumping up and down. 'Do say "yes", Miss Rossall! Do say "yes"!'

Bea shifted Daisy's weight on to one arm and moved closer to Henry Dearden. 'I do say "yes",' she smiled up at him, 'and I won't have to learn to love you – for I already do.'

'If she's comin' back, I'm goin'!' a harsh voice declared from inside the hallway.

Bea and Henry tore their glance from each other and swung round to see Mrs Kellett, dressed in her hat and coat, glaring at them in disgust. A bunch of keys dangled ominously from one hand and a few packed bags lay at her feet. 'This used to be a respectable 'ouse.'

Bea was glad to have Mr Dearden's protective arm around her shoulders.

'It still is, Mrs Kellett,' Henry said mildly. 'Neither I nor Miss Rossall have done anything wrong but, when we are married, we will both adopt Daisy as our own. I am sorry to see you go. However, you must do as your conscience tells you. You have served my family well in the past and I will write you a reference stating such. If you care to wait half an hour or so in the sitting room, I will send Gertie to ask Johnny Gregson to order a cab for you from Livesey's. I will also arrange a night's lodging at the Crown Hotel. Now, if you will hand over your keys to Mrs Hurst, Miss Rossall's former housekeeper, I am sure, she will be delighted to take your place.'

Mrs Hurst's delighted, 'That I will, sir!' drowned out the sound of Mrs Kellett's outraged, 'Well, really!'

New life seemed to surge through Mrs Hurst's body. 'Eeh, come on, childer. Show me t'way t't'kichen, and I'll mek us all a nice cup o' tea. I 'ope you both 'as 'ealthy appetites. You come, too, Nanny Adams. I think we're goin' to be good friends, me an' you.'

As their voices faded away down the hall towards the kitchen, Bea and Henry smiled delightedly into each other's eyes. Neither had expected such a smooth ending to the situation and seemed a little bemused by it. Henry reached out and held her face gently for a moment, the depth of his love revealed in the tenderness of his expression.

He smiled. 'I fell in love with a prim, severe-looking governess – and now I am looking forward to getting to know the real Beatrice Rossall. You are beautiful. You will take the local society by storm. I'll have to keep on my toes to fend off any rivals.'

Bea nestled against him. 'You have no rivals. You're the one

I have fallen in love with. What more could I want? A husband for me – and a father for Daisy.'

The answer was a deep and loving kiss that quite took her breath away.